Children's Literature from Asia in Today's Classrooms

Children's Literature from Asia in Today's Classrooms

Toward Culturally Authentic Interpretations

Edited by
Yukari Takimoto Amos and
Daniel Miles Amos

ROWMAN & LITTLEFIELD
Lanham • Boulder • New York • London

Published by Rowman & Littlefield
An imprint of The Rowman & Littlefield Publishing Group, Inc.
4501 Forbes Boulevard, Suite 200, Lanham, Maryland 20706
www.rowman.com

Unit A, Whitacre Mews, 26-34 Stannary Street, London SE11 4AB

Copyright © 2018 by Yukari Takimoto Amos and Daniel Miles Amos

All rights reserved. No part of this book may be reproduced in any form or by any electronic or mechanical means, including information storage and retrieval systems, without written permission from the publisher, except by a reviewer who may quote passages in a review.

British Library Cataloguing in Publication Information Available

Library of Congress Cataloging-in-Publication Data

Names: Amos, Yukari Takimoto, editor, author. | Amos, Daniel Miles, editor, author. | Johnson, Lauri, writer of foreword.
Title: Children's literature from Asia in today's classrooms : towards culturally authentic interpretations / [edited by] Yukari Takimoto Amos and Daniel Miles Amos.
Description: Lanham : Rowman & Littlefield, 2018. | Includes bibliographical references.
Identifiers: LCCN 2018014480 (print) | LCCN 2018023046 (ebook) | ISBN 9781475843699 (Electronic) | ISBN 9781475843675 (cloth)
Subjects: LCSH: Children's literature—History and criticism—Theory, etc. | Children's literature—Asia—History and criticism. | Children's literature—Asia—Study and teaching. | Children—Books and reading—Asia—Bibliography.
Classification: LCC PN1009.A1 (ebook) | LCC PN1009.A1 C55 2018 (print) | DDC 809/.89282095—dc23
LC record available at https://lccn.loc.gov/2018014480

To our daughter, Himiko (卑弥呼)

Contents

Foreword: Creating Empathy and Equity through Asian International Children's Literature — ix
Lauri Johnson, Boston College

Preface: Globalization and Teacher Education — xi
Yukari Takimoto Amos

Acknowledgments — xvii

Introduction — 1
Daniel Miles Amos

PART I: CLASSROOM APPLICATIONS — 3

1. Gods, Heroes, Wisdom, and Wit in Children's Stories from India — 5
   Anita Balagopalan

2. Thai Cultural References and Decision Making in *The Happiness of Kati* — 17
   Kamolwan Fairee Jocuns

3. Chinese Children Stories, Confucianism, and the Family — 29
   Haiyue (Fiona) Shan with Daniel Miles Amos

4. The Monkey within You: *Journey to the West*, an Essential Text of Chinese Religion and Folk Cosmology — 37
   Daniel Miles Amos

5. Reading *Sadako* with Third Graders — 55
   Trina Lanegan

PART II: ANNOTATED BIBLIOGRAPHIES OF INTERNATIONAL CHILDREN'S LITERATURE FROM SELECTED ASIAN COUNTRIES   71

6   Annotated Bibliographies of International Children's Literature from Selected Asian Countries   73

     China/Taiwan   73
     Miao Ying (Janet) Chen

     Indonesia   77
     Tati Lathipatud Durriyah

     Japan   83
     Yae Takimoto Hite and Katrina Manami Knight

     Philippines   88
     Jordan Piano

     South Korea   93
     Eun Yoo

     Thailand   97
     Kamolwan Fairee Jocuns

About the Editors   101

About the Contributors   103

Foreword

Creating Empathy and Equity through Asian International Children's Literature

Lauri Johnson, Boston College

Twenty-five years ago I directed a program in the New York City schools known as PROJECT EQUAL, which was created to develop empathy and equity through the use of multicultural children's literature (Johnson & Smith, 1993). At the time, my colleagues and I were responding to the rapidly changing demographics in cities across the United States and a wave of interest among educators about how to develop school curriculum, which might be more responsive to the culturally diverse students "sitting in front of them."

We also hoped to reduce prejudice and stereotyping by focusing on fiction, which realistically portrayed the realities of race and racism in the lives of young people. We believed that multicultural literature could serve as both a "window and a mirror" (Bishop, 1990) to help students of color see themselves and their families reflected in the books they read, as well as for white children to enter into the lives of children who experienced different racial realities.

In our work in hundreds of city schools, we learned it was not enough, however, to provide students and teachers with culturally conscious picture books and novels in order to change their hearts and minds. Guided group discussion was needed to mediate and influence students' interpretations of what they read, help dispel stereotypes, and link multicultural literature in thematic units with other areas of the curriculum.

Now fast forward twenty-five years, and today's classrooms in New York City (and other major cities across the United States) are even more diverse, with first- and second-generation Asian and Asian American students one of the fastest growing student populations. And yet there is little evidence that we have expanded the present literary canon in K–16 schools to incorporate the cultural perspectives and traditions of new immigrant students as well as established Asian American communities.

The chapters in this volume focus on international children's literature from India, China, Indonesia, Japan, South Korea, Thailand, and the Philippines, with characters, story lines, and cultural referents that may not be familiar to American K–16 students and teachers.

The selections in this book go a long way, however, illustrating how these cultural referents might inform classroom teaching, from the Confucian values underlying popular Chinese folktales to chronicling the use of *Sadako and the Thousand Paper Cranes* (Coerr, 1977) with a third-grade class in order to develop their knowledge of the aftereffects of the atomic attack on Japan during World War II. The annotated bibliographies in Part II provide particularly helpful interpretations, which situate the story or folktale within that particular country's cultural and religious traditions as well as provide classroom applications and curriculum extensions that relate these stories to other literary traditions.

The thoughtful use of Asian international children's literature can be an important way to develop empathy in both students and teachers alike. As Warren (2018) notes in his recent study of empathy and culturally responsive pedagogy, engaging in perspective taking—adopting the social perspectives of others as an act and process of knowing—invites preservice teachers to develop new knowledge of students and the sociocultural context where she or he will teach. Through critically discussing international Asian children's literature in light of the experiences and realities of students of Asian descent in the United States, students and teachers learn not only how to empathize but also explore how the cultural traditions represented may shift and become hybridized as Asian families become Asian American.

As you read through this interesting volume, I would encourage you to savor and learn from the stories recounted, but also dig deep to challenge your own preconceived notions and consider how these chapters might be used to create empathy and equity in K–12 and university classrooms alike.

REFERENCES

Bishop, R. S. (1990). Mirrors, windows, and sliding glass doors. *Perspectives: Choosing and Using Books for the Classroom*, 6(3), ix–xi.

Coerr, E. (1977). *Sadako and the thousand paper cranes*. New York: Putnam.

Johnson, L., & Smith, S. (1993). *Dealing with diversity through multicultural fiction: Library-classroom partnerships*. Chicago: American Library Association.

Warren, C. (2018). Empathy, teacher dispositions, and preparation for culturally responsive pedagogy. *Journal of Teacher Education*, 69(2), 169–83.

Preface
Globalization and Teacher Education
Yukari Takimoto Amos

Educational institutions in the United States have been recognizing the need to prepare students more adequately for the challenges of globalization. The world has been rapidly interconnecting politically, economically, and culturally and establishing connections through the sharing of information. Developing "globally competent students who are not only more marketable but who are also better prepared to make positive contributions to a global society and who will build a sustainable world" (Simpson & Grimes, 2016, p. 239) is of great importance in higher education.

In US colleges and universities, programs aimed at providing an international perspective and cross-cultural skills are increasingly popular. Hayward and Siaya (2001) report that the public is also supportive of foreign language instruction in higher education, and even more strongly favors courses that focus on international issues.

In teacher education, however, two conflicting ideas seem to coexist. Almost twenty-five years ago, Merryfield (1994) lamented that only about 5 percent of the nation's K–12 teachers have had any academic preparation in global education and that students in teacher education programs take fewer courses with global or international content than do all other college majors. Although study-abroad programs are popular among teacher candidates, it is not uncommon to witness teacher candidates who are profoundly ignorant about other countries, in particular Asia, the Middle East, and Africa.

Gay (2003) accurately states that people who come from Asia and the Middle East are perceived to be holding more unfamiliar cultures and languages compared to immigrants from Western and Northern Europe in the earlier periods and that people hold more biases and anxiety about the people from these countries/regions.

This type of ignorance was displayed in my teacher education class when one female teacher candidate expressed her lack of knowledge of the world. She declared that she was glad to know me and was "happy to learn that not all Japanese are Communists." I responded, "You're probably thinking of China, aren't you? Not all Chinese are Communists, and Japan is not part of China." Without looking embarrassed about her ignorance, she responded, "But I thought Japan is a Communist country. Isn't it part of China?" Sadly enough, this type of ignorance of simple facts is not a rare phenomenon among teacher candidates at my university.

Teacher candidates in US teacher education programs are the byproducts of the US PK–16 education system that we strive to change. Banks (2016) explains why most students have little awareness or understanding of other countries and global issues:

> Most nation-states focus on helping students to develop nationalism rather than to understand their role as citizens of the world. The teaching of nationalism often results in students' learning misconceptions, stereotypes, and myths about other nations and acquiring negative and confused attitudes toward them. (p. 32)

Banks (2016) further adds that many teachers tend to view global education as an add-on to an already crowded curriculum and thus assign it a low priority. Due to the worldwide dominance of the English language and the economic, political, and military power of the United States, US citizens in particular are more vulnerable to being ignorant about other countries. There is a need to prepare US students for global-mindedness. However, the need may not register as imminent to those who are accustomed to the privileges dominance brings.

If we attempt to educate our future students so that they can effectively participate in the globalized world, it is essential that we reform our own PK–16 education system. This is where educating teacher candidates for globalism becomes imperative.

USE OF MULTICULTURAL AND INTERNATIONAL CHILDREN'S LITERATURE IN TEACHER EDUCATION

Frequently, teacher educators introduce children's literature from other countries in their attempt to teach how to effectively use such literature in future classrooms. International children's literature has the potential to create global experiences and cultural insights for children and young adults confronted with the limited and biased images of the world that they may receive from the media (Mathis, 2015).

Therefore, reading stories from other countries allows children and young adults to discover a world beyond their own family and community. In addition, stories from a variety of cultures can raise children's global cultural consciousness. Exposure to international children's literature in the classroom, if sensitive sociocultural and historical context are provided, can have positive effects.

The exposure to international literature will benefit not only children and young adults who read these books in the classroom but also teacher candidates who may have been rarely introduced to such literature in their past education. Simply said, without reading international children's literature themselves, teachers cannot use it effectively in their own classroom. This also corresponds to the tendency that most teacher candidates feel unprepared to teach children from diverse backgrounds (Barksdale et al., 2002).

During teacher preparation, most have not been taught how to embed multicultural, international, and diversity pedagogy into their own future classrooms (Gay, 2010). Considering this reality, the intentional introduction and teaching of how to effectively use international and multicultural children's literature in teacher education is a sound pedagogical strategy for teacher education.

The effects of the use of international and multicultural children's literature on teacher candidates' cultural consciousness and pedagogical improvement have been researched, and these studies found positive effects.

Nathenson-Mejia and Escamilla (2003) found that using Latina/o children's literature in field experience seminars helped white preservice teachers to bridge cultural gaps and broaden their personal perspective and understanding of cultures different from their own. Colby and Lyon (2004) note that teacher candidates had realized how significant their role would be in using multicultural literature in the classroom for the benefit of all students. Iwai (2015) reveals that teacher candidates developed positive attitudes toward multicultural and diversity issues, identified multicultural literature as crucial to foster children's awareness of diversity, and planned to use them in their future classrooms.

Through international and multicultural literature, teacher candidates are encouraged to examine values and attitudes different from their own, and this examination leads to reflective practices. Perhaps the most important effect is that reading international and multicultural literature facilitates teacher candidates' reflection on themselves and others, and as a result can help to change their attitudes and deepen their understanding of cultures other than their own (Cai, 2008).

CONCERNS AND CHALLENGES

The use of multicultural and international literature in teacher education offers teacher candidates opportunities to gain broader understanding about the world and people different from them, and it encourages them to reflect upon their own cultural values. It presents challenges as well. Obtaining high-quality texts is always challenging. Even if teachers want to use certain international children's literature, English translations may not be available.

A more complicated and daunting issue is how teachers select what literature to read in the classroom. Teachers' selection of literature depends on how they interpret it. This point presents a particular challenge to international literature. International literature reflects upon each country, society, and culture's unique values and practices, and it is not usually written for people outside the country of origin. Therefore, it is likely that readers in other countries may not understand those values, or may find such values irrelevant or conflicting with their own. If the readers experience this cultural dissonance, they may end up misreading and misinterpreting the stories.

Potential but likely misinterpretations of international stories by foreign readers have been pointed out in several studies. These studies have particularly highlighted the problematic nature of the incongruence and clash of values between the culture of the book and the readers' culture.

When there is a wide difference in cultural values, the reader may simply "reject or react negatively to literacy work that may have nothing to do with the book's quality as literature" (Freeman & Lehman, 2001, p. 27). This type of resistance or rejection by the reader is called "aesthetic restriction" (Soter, 1997). When aesthetic restriction occurs, the reader may dismiss the work out of hand because of elements in the text that they find unacceptable (Soter, 1997). This is because it is easier for the reader to dismiss and reject a foreign story that they find incomprehensible or unsuitable rather than attempting to understand the story from the foreign other's viewpoint.

Boyd (2002), for example, described a ninth grader's frustration and disappointment with *Chain of Fire*, Beverly Naidoo's (1993) powerful novel about apartheid South Africa, told from the perspective of a black teenage girl who, with members of her family and residents of her town, resists being forcibly removed to a so-called homeland hundreds of miles away. Rice (2005) reported that sixth graders negatively interpreted the work of Gary Soto, a gifted Mexican American poet and author of memoirs and novels, including literature for children, because they were not familiar with the physical appearance, language, and food customs he presented in his stories.

Aesthetic restriction occurs because, as Brindley and Laframboise (2002) warn, "Many preservice teachers come into teacher preparation programs with culturally insular perspectives and do not experience the cognitive dissonance necessary to reexamine their cultural beliefs" (p. 405). Teacher candidates who lack experience with diverse perspectives, both inside and outside the United States, are vulnerable to aesthetic restriction. They may dismiss literature that could provide PK–16 students with the reality that people in other cultures have different perspectives, perspectives that are as important to them as their own.

Ideally, teachers should authentically interpret stories that originate from countries that speak different languages, believe in different religions, and hold different values. Ultimately, this stance represents "respect for others."

REFERENCES

Banks, J. A. (2016). *Cultural diversity and education: Foundations, curriculum, and teaching* (6th ed.). New York: Routledge.

Barksdale, M. A., Richards, J., Fisher, P., Wuthrick, M., Hammons, J., & Grisham, D. (2002). Perceptions of preservice elementary teachers on multicultural issues. *Reading Horizon, 43*(1), 27–48.

Boyd, F. B. (2002). Conditions, concessions, and the many tender mercies of learning through multicultural literature. *Reading Research and Instruction, 42*(1), 58–92.

Brindley, R., & Laframboise, K. L. (2002). The need to do more: Promoting multiple perspectives in preservice teacher education through children's literature. *Teaching and Teacher Education, 18*(4), 405–20.

Cai, M. (2008). Transactional theory and the study of multicultural literature. *Language Arts, 85*(3), 212–20.

Colby, S. A., & Lyon, A. F. (2004). Heightening awareness about the importance of using multicultural literature. *Multicultural Education, 11*(3), 24–28.

Freeman, E. B., & Lehman, B. A. (2001). *Global perspectives in children's literature.* Boston: Pearson/Allyn and Bacon.

Gay, G. (2003). The importance of multicultural education. *Educational Leadership, 61*(4), 30–35.

———. (2010). *Culturally responsive teaching: Theory, research, and practice* (2nd ed.). New York: Teachers College Press.

Hayward, F. M., & Siaya, L. M. (2001). *Public experience, attitudes, and knowledge: A report on two national surveys about international education.* Washington, DC: American Council on Education.

Iwai, Y. (2015). Multicultural children's literature and teacher candidates' awareness and attitudes toward cultural diversity. *International Electronic Journal of Elementary Education, 5*(2), 185–98.

Mathis, J. B. (2015). Demonstrations of agency in contemporary international children's literature: An exploratory critical content analysis across personal, social, and cultural dimensions. *Literacy Research and Instruction, 54*(3), 206–30.

Merryfield, M. (1994). *Teacher education in global & international education.* Washington, DC: American Association of Colleges for Teacher Education.

Nathenson-Mejia, S., & Escamilla, K. (2003). Connecting with Latino children: Bridging cultural gaps with children's literature. *Bilingual Research Journal*, *27*(1), 101–16.

Rice, P. S. (2005). It "ain't" always so: Sixth graders' interpretations of Hispanic-American stories with universal themes. *Children's Literature in Education*, *36*(4), 343–62.

Simpson, T., & Grimes, L. H. (2016). Education abroad co-curricular experiences that result in intercultural responsive leadership growth. In K. Jones & J. R. Mixon (Eds.), *Intercultural responsiveness in the second language learning classroom* (pp. 238–57). Hershey, PA: IGI Global.

Soter, A. O. (1997). Reading literature of other cultures: Some issues in critical interpretation. In T. Rogers & A. O. Soter (Eds.), *Reading across cultures: Teaching literature in a diverse society* (pp. 213–29). New York: Teachers College Press.

CHILDREN'S LITERATURE CITED

Naidoo, B. (1993). *Chain of fire*. Illustrated by E. Velasquez. New York: HarperCollins.

Tsuchiya, Y. (1997). *Faithful elephants: A true story of animals, people, and war*. Illustrated by T. Lewin. Boston: Houghton Mifflin.

Acknowledgments

As in our companion volume, *(Mis)reading Different Cultures: Interpreting International Children's Literature from Asia*, we would like to acknowledge the many people who contributed, directly and indirectly, to the inspiration behind this book. Daniel thanks his late parents, Miles E. Amos and Jean F. Roper Amos, for imbuing him with a love of literature and travel. Thanks are also due to Mrs. Fuller, Daniel's freshmen English professor, who failed his first assignment when he deserved it and in more than one way encouraged him to use his talents to write.

Many friends in Hong Kong have consistently supported Daniel over a forty-year period. Special acknowledgments are due to Mr. But Ho-Ming, public intellectual, for his consistent advice, support, and friendship, and to Mr. Wong Jan-Ping, martial arts master and Chinese physician, for his talents as a teacher, his generosity, and willingness to share his knowledge of Chinese culture and society.

Both Yukari and Daniel are grateful to their talented writer friend, Nerice Gietel, who expressed a sincere interest in this project and also assisted them in finding potential contributing authors for the book. Both were amazed with Nerice's wide network of scholars and by her ability to convene them quickly. This ability must surely be due to her warm and kind personality, and her deep insight into the strengths and weaknesses of fellow human beings.

Daniel's writing of this book has also been made possible by a Fulbright research grant in Hong Kong, 2017–2018. Yukari completed this book while in Hong Kong during her sabbatical. Thanks go to Central Washington University for granting her the time to concentrate on writing.

Special thanks goes to Susanne Canavan, who discovered the book's potential at an AERA annual meeting in Washington, D.C. Susanne left

Rowman & Littlefield in the middle of the project, but without her this book may not have been written.

Y. T. A.
D. M. A.
Hong Kong

Introduction
Daniel Miles Amos

This book aims to provide the reader with interpretation guides and practical ideas when they endeavor to make use of Asian international children's literature for the classroom. As was explored in the accompanying volume titled *(Mis)reading Different Cultures: Interpreting International Children's Literature from Asia*, stories that originate from different cultures and countries can, for many reasons, be misinterpreted.

This volume attempts to help the reader interpret stories from Asia more authentically, and it focuses on international children's literature and international literature read by young adults. Despite growing Asian populations in Western nations and the increasing influence that Asian countries hold in the world in the political, social, and cultural domains, Asian international children's literature is still a relatively unexamined field in Western education. In an increasingly interconnected world, understanding Asian international children's literature from a variety of Asian cultural perspectives and effectively using it in the classroom are necessary and worthy goals for PK–16 classrooms and teacher education programs.

The book is divided into two parts. Part I discusses how to authentically read children's literature from four countries: India, Thailand, China, and Japan. These chapters provide a guide for meaningful interpretations of cultural aspects of children's stories from these countries that can help outside readers comprehend the stories accurately.

In chapter 1, Anita Balagopalan discusses how Hinduism and the cultural values of India are interwoven in the stories commonly told to children. Many stories for children in India are derived from Hindu epics.

For example, the *Mahābhārata*, an ancient epic poem, combines beautiful literature with engaging stories, and it is a work that is essential to Hindu religious philosophy. Balagopalan presents stories from the first chapter of the

Mahābhārata: *Devavrata*, and introduces the concepts of karma and karmic retribution, reincarnation, and dharma (roughly translated as "duty"). Other stories introduce major Hindu gods and heroes, as well as the cultural value put on wit, humor, and intelligence, such as that found in *Two Thieves* from *The Great Tenali Rama: Stories of Wits and Humor*.

Kamolwan Fairee Jocuns invites the reader to the world of *Kati*, an award-winning novel about a nine-year-old Thai girl, in chapter 2. The Thai cultural references discussed by Jocuns include detailed cultural explanations that can prevent non-Thai readers from misreading and misinterpreting this popular Thai children's story. This chapter reminds us that whenever we read a translated version of an international story, we may miss the story's cultural significance.

In chapter 3, Haiyue (Fiona) Shan and Daniel Miles Amos introduce Confucianism, an ancient but still profoundly significant philosophy in East Asian cultures. Using stories widely read by Chinese parents and children, Shan and Amos explain how various ideas of Confucianism are intertwined within the stories.

Daniel Miles Amos discusses the classic Chinese novel *Journey to the West* (*Monkey King*), and its influence on the development of Chinese folk beliefs and religious cosmology, in chapter 4. He provides several examples of contemporary Chinese religious beliefs and activity related to the novel so that readers might understand the nature of Chinese religion and more fully comprehend the story.

In chapter 5, Trina Lanegan carefully re-enacts an event from her third-grade classroom. She delineates how her third graders interpreted the story of a Japanese girl, *Sadako*, who died of leukemia shortly after World War II and how she as a teacher responded to her students' interpretations. The way Lanegan taught the lesson can be emulated by other teachers. The dilemmas Lanegan felt with regard to her children's interpretations are frequently experienced by other teachers when they teach stories that originate from other cultures.

Part II consists of annotated bibliographies of international children's literature from selected Asian societies: China, Taiwan, Indonesia, Japan, South Korea, the Philippines, and Thailand. The detailed summaries and faithful interpretations of each story from these societies can be used by teachers to prepare lessons with greater cultural authenticity.

All the chapters are meant for a practical usage and to encourage accurate interpretations of international children's literature from Asia. For this reason, anyone who is engaged in reading stories from Asia is encouraged to explore the volume. The editors particularly want readers to avoid misinterpreting stories with which they are not familiar, and hope that they will find each author's cultural insights fascinating and useful as they attempt to read with cultural authenticity.

Part I

CLASSROOM APPLICATIONS

Chapter 1

Gods, Heroes, Wisdom, and Wit in Children's Stories from India

Anita Balagopalan

Stories that are essential to Hindu religion, mythology, and wisdom are commonly told to children in India. Many stories are derived from the *Mahābhārata,* an ancient epic poem of great length, which combines beautiful literature with engaging plots and lessons for children and adults alike.

Ganesha, a story from Hindu mythology, describes the strength but also the humanlike weaknesses of Hindu gods, as well as the birth of the beloved elephant-headed god of the same name. It, too, serves as the source of children's stories.

Other children's stories from India are inspired by beloved historical figures, such those based on the wit, wisdom, and humor of Tenali Ramakrishna, a legendary sixteenth-century Telugu poet and scholar.

Authentic comprehension of these stories requires one to understand important concepts in Hinduism, such as karma, rebirth, and dharma. Using popular children's stories read in India, this chapter delineates these concepts.

BIRTH OF A HERO: *DEVAVRATA* FROM THE *MAHĀBHĀRATA*

The *Mahābhārata* is a complex story, full of plots and subplots, and has been passed down through generations in India. Among the many versions that exist of this epic, C. Rajagopalachari's is widely accepted as one of the best, especially for children. Rajaji, as he was fondly called, was an eminent Indian politician, the last governor-general of India, a great scholar and author.

The *Mahābhārata* is one of the two great epic poems of Hindu religion and literature; the other being *The Ramayana* (which, as mentioned by D. M. Amos in chapter 4 of this volume, influenced the characterization

Monkey in the Chinese novel *Journey to the West*). The *Mahābhārata* is traditionally ascribed to Vyasa, a revered figure in Hindu tradition (Fowler, 2012).

SUMMARY OF THE STORY

The first chapter of the *Mahābhārata* begins when the great king, Shantanu, becomes besotted with a beautiful woman and asks her to marry him, not realizing that she is the great goddess Ganga, in human form. Ganga agrees to marry Shantanu on the condition that he will neither ask her about her background nor question any of her actions. The infatuated king agrees.

The couple lives happily, and Ganga gives birth to many babies. However, Shantanu is horrified every time Ganga gives birth, as she throws each newborn into the river as soon as he or she is born. Remembering his promise, Shantanu asks her no questions. Ganga drowns seven children, but when the eighth child is born, Shantanu can no longer bear it. He asks her to explain her terrifying behavior.

Ganga then explains who she really is, and why she has been drowning her newborns. The great sage Vasishtha had put a curse on eight Vasus, or elemental deities, and caused them to be reincarnated as mortals because they stole his cow. When the eight Vasus apologized and begged for forgiveness, Vasishtha reduced their sentences to less than a year of mortal life, except for Prabhasa, the one who had actually stolen the cow. The Vasus then approached Ganga and asked her to be their mother when they were reincarnated. They begged Ganga to kill them as soon as they were born so that they would not have to suffer the painful lives of mortals.

Because Shantanu broke his vow to Ganga, she prepares to leave him and disappear with the eighth child, who is a reincarnation of Prabhasa. Before leaving, Ganga promises Shantanu that she will bring the child up well and return with him after some years. After losing Ganga, Shantanu gives up all worldly pleasures and lived as an ascetic king. Sixteen years later, while walking along the banks of the River Ganga, he sees a beautiful young boy making a dam of arrows across the river. Ganga reappears and says that this is his son, Devavrata, and she has brought him up to be a master of arms, arts, sciences, and governance. She blesses the boy, hands him to his father, and disappears once again.

Devavrata goes on to become Bhishma, a central character in the *Mahābhārata*, who lives a long life and is worshipped by all for his nobility, sacrifice, and unwavering sense of duty.

KARMA AND REBIRTH

The story of Devavrata exemplifies karma and rebirth. In Hinduism, karma and rebirth are important concepts.

Karma refers to the spiritual principle of cause and effect, where a person's actions are the cause for what will happen to them in the future. Rebirth or reincarnation means that life is infinite and goes on in one form or another. Though different concepts, the two are closely intertwined because one could face the consequences of his/her actions in the present life or in the next birth. In fact, the next birth itself could depend on one's karma and could mean being born again either as a higher life form or a lower one.

No one is above the concept of karma and rebirth, not even the gods. They, too, are held accountable for their actions, and they can die and be reborn, depending on their karma.

The Vasus were gods themselves, but they indulged in a petty theft. Thus, they brought bad karma on themselves. Similar to Greek mythology, gods mingle freely with humans, sages, and demons. They also display the same virtues and vices at different points in life. Because of the Vasus' theft, they were cursed to be reborn as humans. A life of mortal suffering and less power is a significant step down for gods. By apologizing and repenting wholeheartedly, they were able to get Vasishtha to reduce their sentence to less than a year as mortals.

Ganga, although appearing to be an unnatural and cruel mother, was actually helping the Vasus by agreeing to give birth to them and release them from their reincarnated lives as humans.

Prabhasa, however, was condemned to a long life as a human. Vasishtha forgave him slightly and made a concession: although it would be long, his life as a human would be bright and illustrious. The analogy is that of the sun—an object that burns brightly, gives the world light, and gets nothing in return. This act is the ultimate karmic retribution and would allow Prabhasa to be cleansed of all his sins. That is why Devavrata went on to become Bhishma in *Mahābhārata*, a central character who remains great and unsullied, never marries, and instead dedicates himself to the service of his brothers' families and the kingdom.

Readers must understand that karma is not the same as a curse or sentence. Usually, the act of a sage or a god cursing someone is more like a teacher imparting a hard lesson to his or her students. It helps them understand what they have done wrong and accept the consequence of their actions or their own karma. Negative karma can be lessened with severe penance and sincere repentance, but it can never be lifted completely because it is, after all, a consequence of a person's own actions.

BHISHMA'S VOW FROM THE *MAHĀBHĀRATA*

Chapter 2 of the *Mahābhārata* is called *Bhishma's Vow*. After Devavrata returns to the kingdom with his father, he is rightfully crowned heir to the throne. Four years later, King Shantanu sees and falls in love with the daughter of the chief of the fishermen. He wants to marry her and approaches her father for her hand in marriage. The shrewd fisherman agrees, on the condition that her son will become king after Shantanu.

King Shantanu cannot agree to this because Devavrata is already the crown prince. He returns to his palace and languishes away in silence. His son asks him what the matter is, and he tells him half-truths, saying he is worried about the continuance of the family line because he has only one son.

Devavrata realizes that his father is lying and finds out the truth from the king's charioteer. He then goes to the fisherman and asks for his daughter's hand for his father. The fisherman wants assurance that neither Devavrata nor his sons will claim the throne and that his grandson will eventually be crowned king.

Devavrata then renounces his claim to the throne, takes a vow of chastity, and promises he will never marry. As he utters these words, the gods shower flowers on his head and cries of "Bhishma" are heard. *Bhishma* means "one who makes a terrible vow but fulfills it." That is how Devavrata comes to be known as Bhishma. He remains loved and respected by everyone in the kingdom for his integrity, sense of duty, and his ultimate sacrifice.

KARMIC SACRIFICE AND DHARMA

This story could appear as unnatural and unrealistic to non-Indian readers. After all, it is about a son in the prime of his youth, taking a vow of unbroken chastity so that his lustful father may marry a beautiful young woman. Not only that, he also hands over his rightful place as heir to the throne to their future children.

In India the unfairness of the situation is not lost on the readers, and this only makes Bhishma more of a tragic-heroic character. In Hinduism, making a vow of austerity and chastity, and then fulfilling it, is considered to be the greatest sacrifice possible. That along with undisturbed prayer and penance makes a person eligible for the highest reward from gods, sages, and kings. After making his terrible vow, Devavrata could have asked to be liberated from his mortal life, but he did not, because it was his karmic retribution to live a long and illustrious life and give up everything in the service of his family and kingdom.

Another concept that needs to be fully understood is the concept of dharma, or duty. In Hindu philosophy, one is expected to do one's duties with no expectation of reward. It was Devavrata's duty to take care of his kingdom and family. Pleased with his son's great sacrifice, Shantanu blessed him with the power to choose the time of his own death. Knowing that the people of the kingdom of Hastinapur were unhappy that he would not be king, Bhishma then swore to choose death only after Hastinapur was in safe hands. Until then, he would remain its loyal servant.

Bhishma remained devoted to his duty or dharma until his death. On his deathbed, he stayed alive for fifty-eight days to give instructions on statesmanship and the performing of duties to Yudhishtir, who then went on to become the next king of Hastinapur. When he finally decided to choose death, he attained salvation due to a lifetime of duty, nobility, and sacrifice.

DEATH OF A HERO: *THE PASSING OF BHISHMA* FROM THE *MAHĀBHĀRATA*

Chapter 73 of the *Mahābhārata*, *The Passing of Bhishma*, describes the death of the hero.

On the tenth day of the battle of the *Mahābhārata*, Arjuna, the chief warrior on the side of the Pandavas, rides into battle with Sikhandin in front of him. Sikhandin was born a woman, daughter to King Drupada, but she has transformed herself into a man while living in the forest and perfecting her fighting skills. Arjuna and Sikhandin are targeting Bhishma, who is fighting on behalf of the Kauravas. Bhishma is vehemently against this war between the families of cousins—the Pandavas and the Kauravas. While the Pandavas are noble and worthy to be rulers, it is Bhishma's dharma, or duty, to fight for the Kauravas as they are the rulers of Hastinapur.

While in battle, Bhishma refuses to fight a woman because it is unworthy of a noble warrior. Arjuna keeps himself shielded by Sikhandin and shoots arrows at Bhishma, striking him at furious pace.

Covered in arrows, Bhishma falls, but his body does not reach the ground because it is covered in so many arrows. He lays suspended on a bed of arrows while his head is hanging down. Both armies stop fighting and gather around him. A few of the princes rush to get him a cushion. Bhishma rejects the cushion and asks Arjuna for a cushion for his head, befitting of a warrior. Arjuna puts three arrows into the ground that support his head. He then asks for water. Arjuna shoots an arrow deep into the ground and gets a great fountain of water gushing out to quench Bhishma's thirst.

Bhishma calls for Duryodhana, the eldest brother and leader of the Kauravas, and shows him how Arjuna is caring for him despite having injured him.

He says that he will not let himself die until the sun turns north, but he advises Duryodhana to make peace with his cousins and end the war before his death. Duryodhana refuses to do so. Bhishma stays alive for fifty-eight days on the bed of arrows, choosing to die only when he acknowledges that Hastinapur is in safe hands.

DHARMA AND SUBPLOTS TO BHISHMA'S DEATH

The subplots of the *Mahābhārata* make a linear narration difficult. To understand the background to Bhishma's death, we have to digress into a subplot. After Bhishma's father, King Shantanu, died, Bhishma had to support the king's wife and sons. After one son died childless, it was imperative to get good wives for the other son to ensure the continuity of the family line. Annoyed at a perceived insult to the kingdom of Hastinapur for not being invited to a groom-choosing ceremony known as Swayamvara in the neighboring kingdom of Kashi, Bhishma abducted three of its princesses to be brides for his half-brother.

One princess, Amba, was in love with the prince of another kingdom. Realizing this, Bhishma apologized and allowed her to return to him. But to her horror, she found that neither her lover nor Bhishma's half-brother was willing to accept her anymore. In despair, she begged Bhishma to marry her, but he refused because of his vow. Furious and dishonored, she lived in poverty and deep prayer for years until the gods granted her the wish to be able to kill Bhishma. She was promised that she would be able to do it in her next rebirth. Impatient for revenge, she killed herself and was reborn as the daughter of Drupada, who then went on to become Sikhandin.

Bhishma made many mistakes in his life. Abducting the three princesses of Kashi was one of the biggest mistakes, and it was one for which he paid with his life. It was his karma. Bhishma recognized Sikhandin as Amba, the princess he had abducted. He also knew that she had been granted the power to kill him. But he did not step away from his dharma, which was to fight on behalf of Hastinapur. Noble to the very end, he stuck to his vow of not choosing death until the kingdom was in safe hands.

After the battle was over and the Pandavas had won, Bhishma transferred his knowledge of good governance and dharma to Yudhishtir, the eldest son and leader of the Pandavas. Yudhishtir was exceptionally noble and also known as Dharmaputra, which means "the son of Dharma," so he was known to be devoted to his duties. With Yudhishtir as the ruler of Hastinapur, Bhishma could finally give up his life and attain salvation.

Extreme devotion to duty at the cost of one's life may seem irrational to Western readers, and indeed, many youngsters in India would agree.

However, the tragic-heroic nature of Bhishma still commands profound respect. To this day, rituals respecting him as Bhishma-Pitamah (Bhishma the Patriarch) are performed on his death anniversary according to the Hindu calendar by some families who have lost their own fathers.

THE BELOVED ELEPHANT-HEADED GOD, *GANESHA*

Shiva, one of the three gods in the Hindu trinity, has a large number of ganas, or attendants. One day, his wife, goddess Parvati, asked his chief attendant not to allow anyone into her palace as she was going for a bath. A little later, Shiva strode in, unchecked by the attendant because he is Parvati's husband.

This infuriated Parvati, and she decided to build a gana for herself who would be loyal only to her. She took the sandal paste that she had smeared on her body and used it to mold the figure of a boy. She then blessed him and gave him life. Born from her body, he was now her devoted son.

A few days later, she gave him the same instructions—no one was to be allowed in. Shiva appeared some time later, was refused entry, and was furious, but the boy held his ground. Shiva then asked his ganas to attack the boy, but he fights and defeats all of them. Shiva then summoned the god Brahma along with some wise sages and asked them to reason with the boy. But the boy stood firm. Insulted and keen to teach the insolent boy a lesson, Shiva called his son, Kartikeya, and the god Indra, and asked them to battle with the boy.

Again, the boy held his ground. Hearing the commotion and realizing what Shiva had done, Parvati was furious that he had ordered an attack on her son. She created two fierce avatars of herself, Kali and Durga, and sent them to help her son. Together, these three decimated the army of the gods.

The time came for Shiva himself to join the attack, but he was blinded by rage and had lost sight of the principles of war. He attacked the boy from behind and cut off his head. While the ganas and gods celebrated, Shiva felt deeply ashamed of what he had done. On the death of her son, Parvati vowed to kill all the ganas and gods, created an army of avatars of herself, and started swallowing all the ganas and gods.

The gods and ganas begged for mercy, and Parvati relented on the condition that her son would be brought back to life and be granted an honorable status among them. Shiva then ordered his ganas to bring the head of the first creature they found. They came back with an elephant head, and with the blessings of the gods the boy was brought back to life with an elephant head.

Shiva begged for forgiveness and accepted the boy as his own son. Keeping to the agreement, the boy was made leader (*esh*) of the ganas and came to be known as Ganesha.

IMPERFECT AND HUMANLIKE GODS

In regard to stories for children, this is one that may outrage the sensibilities of Western readers due to its violent imagery. But in India, Ganesha the elephant-headed god is so widely adored, even by non-Hindus such as Jains and Buddhists, that everything about him, even the violent way in which he came into existence, is popular.

As mentioned earlier, Hindu gods are far from perfect. Almost all of them suffer from wild tempers. As Shiva himself mentions in his apology to Parvati, arrogance is characteristic of males. Hindu gods are seen as all-powerful and yet all-forgiving. They grant wishes or mete out punishment easily and are moved by the power of prayer, irrespective of the seeker. In turn, most Hindus are also able to love and revere their gods, despite their flaws.

In stories of Hindu mythology and in actual social practice, most women are submissive to their husbands. In the case of Shiva and Parvati, though, the same divine force flows through them, thus she matches her husband in power and temper. When she assumes the avatar of Parvati, she is loving and indulgent, like a mother. Her avatars of Kali and Durga are when she is at her fiercest.

Kali is portrayed as dark skinned, having wild eyes, her tongue sticking out with a garland of human heads and holding a severed head in one hand. It is said that when Kali is awakened, Shiva himself must calm down to keep the balance of nature. Durga is another fierce form of Parvati. She is a warrior goddess and rides into battle on a tiger, holding weapons of destruction in her ten hands. The forms of Kali and Durga were awakened in Parvati when her son was under attack and came from her extreme maternal instinct to protect her young son.

Shiva is portrayed as a very gentle, gullible, and generous god. But because he is the Destroyer, he has a deadly temper and power. Ganesha instinctively recognized that the whole battle was an overreaction. Parvati overreacted to Shiva entering her palace; Shiva overreacted about not being allowed in; and it was just a series of negative events that went on from there. In fact, Ganesha even asked Parvati whether Shiva should be allowed in, but she was unnecessarily adamant about it. Ganesha was created to obey his mother's every demand, and he did so. But he had the wisdom and grace to forgive Shiva and accept him as his father.

Despite their rocky start, Shiva is a good father to Ganesha. Shiva and Parvati already have an elder son, Kartikeya, and they bring up Ganesha as his younger brother. Stories of Ganesha and Kartikeya's sibling rivalry and how Ganesha outwits him each time also make for very popular folktales.

This kind of family bond and reverence for the parents is not uncommon in Indian mythological stories, and until recently, it has been true of Indian society as well. Most Indian children believe that parents are equal to

God and all elders must be respected. In the joint family system, where there are multiple branches of the same family living together, decisions made by the oldest family member will be obeyed by everyone in the household. In younger generations, though, this is fast changing. However, even the most rebellious child will believe that love and respect for elders and parents are much-admired virtues.

That is one of the most endearing qualities of Ganesha. He is loved for his fun-loving nature and devotion to his parents. He loves to eat and is always portrayed with a big stomach. He is obedient and intelligent and finds the smartest way to overcome obstacles. He is the god that everyone prays to before starting any new enterprise. This story is always narrated to young children as an example of how it is necessary to keep one's word to one's parents, even if under attack.

THE TWO THIEVES FROM *THE GREAT TENALI RAMA*

One day in Vijayanagara in Andhra Pradesh, India, two thieves were caught and sent to prison by the royal guards. After a few days, the king visited the thieves in prison but found them unrepentant. So he came up with an idea to teach them a lesson. He promised them freedom if they could steal from his favorite court jester and poet, Tenali Rama, without being caught or outwitted. The thieves believed it would an easy task and went to Tenali Rama's house that night.

Tenali Rama, realizing there were thieves lurking outside, put on an act for them. In front of the thieves he instructed his wife to bundle up their jewelry into a cloth and throw it into the well to keep it safe from thieves who were on the loose. In reality, he only had a box of stones thrown into the well. The thieves drew water from the well the entire night in their effort to get to the jewels. In the morning, Tenali Rama walked up to them and thanked them for watering his garden through the night. The thieves realized they had been outwitted and were pardoned on the condition that they would never steal again.

THE KING'S TRUSTED ADVISOR

Tenali Rama stories are based on a legendary Telugu poet and scholar who lived in the sixteenth century, Tenali Ramakrishna. Ramakrishna was one of the eight poets (Ashtadiggajas) of the court of Sri Krishnadevaraya, the king of Vijayanagara. Ramakrishna had humble beginnings and little formal education. However, he made his way into the court, and thanks to his wit and humor he won the friendship of the king. Ultimately, he was given the title of *vikata-kavi*, which means "court jester and poet" (Dalal, 2014). Tenali Ramakrishna composed works on Hinduism and was a scholar of several languages including Sanskirt, Telugu, Marathi, Tamil, and Kannada (Dalal, 2014).

In India, men of intelligence are often a perfect foil to powerful, sometimes arrogant kings. Their honesty would win the king's confidence, their wisdom would help the king rule fairly and stay in touch with the needs of the ordinary people, and their wit would make their advice palatable to the king. In time, these courtiers have become as famous as the kings themselves, and their stories have been passed down as fables and folklores through generations in India.

Tenali Rama from the court of Sri Krishnadevaraya, Birbal in the court of the Mughal emperor Akbar (sixteenth century), and also Chanakya, the teacher and guide for the greatest Indian emperor, Chandragupta Maurya (fourth century BC), are examples of these highly revered, intelligent men whose sayings and witticisms have become legendary.

CONCLUDING REMARKS

Similar to many other cultures, India's stories for children are inspired by the works of humorists, as well as by religious texts and myths. Hinduism, the principle religion of India, is wonderfully complex, there being numerous schools, concepts, texts, practices, saints, gurus, and philosophers.

In some Hindu traditions there are thirty-three main deities, although in reality everything in the universe can be thought of as part of an interconnected Oneness (Dalal, 2014). Many schools of Hinduism believe that there are millions of deities, or 33 million, or 330 million, with the great majority being female goddesses (Foulston & Abbott, 2009). Indian children's stories introduce elementary concepts of this complex religious philosophy, in addition to bringing entertainment and cultivating an appreciation of a vast and profoundly important world literary tradition.

REFERENCES

Dalal, R. (2014). *Hinduism: An alphabetical guide*. London: Penguin Books.
Foulston, L., & Abbott, S. (2009). *Hindu goddesses: Beliefs and practices*. East Sussex, UK: Sussex Academic Press.
Fowler, J. (2012). *The Bhagavad Gita: A text and commentary for students*. East Sussex, UK: Sussex Academic Press.
Fuller, C. J. (2004). *The Camphor flame: Popular Hinduism and society in India*. Princeton, NJ: Princeton University Press.

CHILDREN'S LITERATURE CITED

Chandrakant, K. (2017). *Ganesha*. Illustrated by C. M. Vitankar. Mumbai, India: Amar Chitra Katha Pvt. Ltd.

Rajagopalachari, C. (2015). *Mahabharata*. Mumbai, India: Bharatiya Vidya Bhavan.

Sufiyan. (2015). *The great Tenali Rama: Stories of wits and humor*. India: Vyanst.

Chapter 2

Thai Cultural References and Decision Making in *The Happiness of Kati*

Kamolwan Fairee Jocuns

This chapter discusses elements of Thai culture that emerge in the children's fiction book *The Happiness of Kati*. In addition, the chapter also analyzes and elaborates on Thai cultural references in the story that give a significant influence on how the characters make certain decisions. Though reader response suggests that readers can create meaning through interpretation based on their own experiences, by exploring Thai cultural references in this chapter, readers can gain alternative and more authentic interpretations of the story.

THE HAPPINESS OF KATI

The Happiness of Kati is a Thai children's novel written by Jane Vejjajiva (Vejjajiva, 2006; เวชชาชีวะ 2550). The book won the South East Asia Writer award in 2006, which is given to talented writers in ten South East Asian countries (Brunei, Cambodia, Indonesia, Laos, Malaysia, Myanmar, the Philippines, Singapore, Thailand, and Vietnam).

The Happiness of Kati is the first book in a trilogy and is the only title in the series that has been translated into English. The translation, completed by Prudence Borthwick, received second prize in the John Dryden Translation Competition organized by the University of East Anglia and the British Comparative Literature Association in 2005.

As a result of the book's interest and popularity (an extended book and a comic) it was made into a movie, book. The movie was made in Thailand in 2009. In 2016, the extended book from the trilogy under the title *Khwam Suk Khong Kati: Ter Khue Khong Khwan* (*The Happiness of Kati: You Are the Gift*) was released. In 2017, a Thai comic book version of *The Happiness of Kati* illustrated by Wisut Ponnimit was published.

The Happiness of Kati is the story of Kati, a nine-year-old girl who has been raised by her grandparents in the countryside of Ayutthaya Province, just north of Bangkok, Thailand. Ayutthaya is the old capital of Siam (the former name of Thailand) and is now one of Thailand's famous tourist attractions and historical sites. The area where Kati and her grandparents live is set far from the busy tourist sites and is quite rural. Their home is a traditional Thai wooden house by a canal, a tranquil area surrounded by the shade of trees.

The novel is divided into three parts: the home on the water, the home by the sea, and the home in the city. The first part chronicles *Kati* and her grandparents' life routine. In the second part Kati sees her mother, and the last part tells about Kati's discovery of her mother's secret and Kati's decision.

Kati is a lively girl who is loved by her grandparents and the people around her. However, behind her happy face she always misses her mother, and she is curious about her mother's absence from her life. The first part of the story does not tell readers about Kati's mother, but there are subheadings in each chapter that reflect Kati's thoughts toward her mother, such as, "Mother never promised to return" (p. 1), "Kati waited every day for Mother" (p. 4)," and "In the house there were no photos of Mother" (p. 8).

Kati enjoys a seemingly plain and simple everyday life at a house by a canal in Ayutthaya. She wakes up to her grandmother's clatter of a spatula against a pan, does daily merit food offerings to the monks, and goes to school with her lunch box nicely prepared by her grandmother. In her free time, she helps her grandmother with the house chores in the kitchen, and she goes on a boat trip along the canal with her grandfather.

One day, Kati eventually gets to see her mother, who lives in a different part of the country at a house by the sea, where Kati/her mother discovers that she is terminally ill with the degenerative disease amyotrophic lateral sclerosis (ALS). As the story unfolds, readers learn that Kati gets to know more about her mother's past, both happy and painful. She learns about her mother's sickness and the incident that made her mother leave her with her grandparents.

Kati's time with her mother in the story is fleeting as her mother is terminally ill. Her mother soon passes away peacefully at the hospital. After the funeral, Uncle Dong, a relative and close friend of Kati's mother, takes Kati to her mother's apartment in Bangkok. Kati finds out more about her mother's past from Uncle Dong. She learns that her father is Burmese and grew up in England.

Her parents were married in England, but the marriage did not last. Uncle Dong gives Kati a letter that her mother left for her. The letter is written to her father. Kati then must decide whether to send the letter to the father she has never met or continue on with her "happiness" without him.

The Happiness of Kati is the first of its trilogy, and some parts in the story are left intentionally ambiguous. For example, Why did Kati's mother leave her husband? This secret is revealed in the second book, *Khwam Suk Khong Kati: Tam Ha Pra Chan* (*The Happiness of Kati: Finding the Moon*), when Kati finds a cassette tape her mother left for her in the apartment in Bangkok. As she listens to the tape, she finds out that her father had an affair with his ex-lover in England while her mother was working in Hong Kong. Her mother left her father on the day she saw him with his ex-lover at her own flat.

LOST IN TRANSLATION

On the surface, *The Happiness of Kati* is a typical children's story where a child character is loved and supported by her family. The overall story line is not difficult to understand by non-Thai readers. However, readers need a number of Thai cultural references in order to deepen their understanding of the cultural traits that the author portrays, some of which are glossed over by the English translation.

Because of the prestigious award that this book received, *The Happiness of Kati* has drawn some analytical attention from Thai researchers, which mostly focus on the translation methods of cultural references and whether the translation has had equivalent effects (Attanatho, 2010; Aungsuwan, 2007).

The studies found that the translator used a number of methods to translate Thai cultural elements, many of which do not have exact equivalent words in English. Because of this, readers with no Thai cultural background may run a risk of misinterpretation. Thai cultural elements that do not have exact equivalent words in English are likely to negatively impact how readers understand the story. Therefore, it is important for readers to have some knowledge about Thai culture in order to understand the story authentically, such as why a certain incident happens in the story and why some certain elements appear.

The remainder of this chapter draws attention to Kati and her mother's choices of action that are tied to Thai culture and beliefs that non-Thai readers will likely misinterpret or simply not understand. The chapter is organized by the following discussion topics: Mother's decision in relation to animism, Kati's decision in pursuit of happiness, and the meaning of happiness in the countryside.

MOTHER'S DECISION AND ANIMISM

Some readers may think that the story is influenced by Thai Buddhism. For example, "Although written entirely in a Thai Buddhist context it should appeal to young (and not so young) readers of all backgrounds and faiths as the theme is universal—finding true happiness in spite of adversity" (Mayosmith, 2006, para. 1).

Thailand indeed adheres to Buddhism. The vast majority (approximately 93 percent) are Buddhists, but animistic worship is also prevalent alongside Buddhism. Animism is a form of religious practice in which the world of spirits and the world of humans are intertwined. Thai animism involves making a vow to supernatural beings and also has a significant impact on the decision one of the characters makes in the book.

In the chapter "Frangipani," after Kati reunites with her mother at the house by the sea, her mother tells stories from the day Kati was born until the incident that separated them. After Kati's mother is diagnosed with ALS, she goes to live with her parents at the home on the water in Ayutthaya. At that time she still cannot accept that she has an incurable disease.

One day she takes her four-year-old daughter, Kati, out for a rowboat trip, and on the way back they get stuck in a storm. Kati's mother suddenly begins to experience a symptom from the disease and struggles to help her daughter out of the boat. She cries out for help but realizes nobody can hear her. She decides to make a wish to all sacred things. She makes a vow that if her daughter makes it safe out of the storm, she will never touch her daughter again:

> You could say I made a promise to all things sacred that if there were such things as miracles, please keep my daughter safe and I would give up everything I owned, everything. Most people would say they'd give their life in exchange but I, of course, had very little life left to give. The sky split with lightning as if acknowledging my promise: if my child was safe, then I would never so much as touch her again. I would go far away from my child and never bring her into danger again. (Vejjajiva, 2006, pp. 60–61)

Normally, Thai people would go to a specific place to make a wish and give a vow. If they cannot be at the place where the sacred things are located, they would make a wish to a specific sacred thing in their mind. However, it is not clear what "all sacred things" Kati's mother refers to. Throughout the book she does not show whether she has a belief of a specific sacred thing. The sacred things she makes a vow to could be anything that is available at that time and place. They could be spirits in the trees, spirits in the houses nearby, or gods in the sky.

In Thai animism, when one makes a wish, he/she will also promise to offer something in return. Once the wish is fulfilled, he/she has to do what he/she has promised. If not, he/she will encounter more bad luck. The offering could be anything—food, money, or any action that an individual believes is worthy of reciprocating for his/her wish. In Kati's mother's case, she trades the safety of Kati with her promise not to touch her again.

This type of belief is an old village belief that came before the spread of Buddhism in Thailand and is still deeply rooted among many Thais, even those who grew up in the city like Kati's mother.

Kriengkraipetch (2000) studied supernatural beliefs in one village in Thailand and found that there are two types of spirits: malevolent and benevolent spirits, although the distinction is not clear-cut. The benevolent spirits help and protect people and in return they receive sacrifices and offerings. However, if one offends or behaves improperly toward the benevolent spirits (e.g., not giving an offering or paying respect to the spirit), the spirits will turn malevolent and harm that person.

It is important to understand that Kati's mother does not abandon her daughter but keeps her promise to the supernatural being. It is risky not to keep the promise because she would never know what harm she or Kati would be exposed to from defying the supernatural being. A promise to a supernatural being is not something to take lightly because it impacts the decision Kati's mother makes, and that decision changes both Kati's and her mother's life.

Kati and her mother get out of the storm by the help of a young boy named Tong who later becomes Kati's best friend. Tong is introduced in the first chapter of the book as an abbot's pupil and nephew. In the Thai version, Kati refers to him as Pee-Tong, which means older (brother) Tong. On that stormy day, Tong is out on the boat in search of Kati and finds them stuck in the storm. His boat appears just after lightning has struck, immediately after Kati's mother has asked for help from the supernatural being. The story suggests that Tong has been sent by sacred forces to help Kati and her mother.

However, even though Kati's mother knows Tong as "the knight in shining armor who had saved little Kati's life" (Vejjajiva, 2006, p. 63), she also holds on to her superstitious belief. The following morning, as narrated in the next chapter of the novel, she leaves without saying a word:

> That night Kati took ill with a fever. The family had to sit up with her all night, bathing her with damp cloths. It was nearly dawn before her fever abated. As the morning light broke, Mother packed her bags and left the little house on the water without saying goodbye, never to return. (p. 64)

The grandparents do not know why their daughter made such a decision. Even though they were very sad about her leaving, they did not ask why or held her back. They only respected her decision and hoped one day she would tell them why.

Readers using rational, nonsupernatural perspectives might question why she leaves Kati. To them it would be obvious that they were saved from the storm by the help of Tong, not by a supernatural miracle. They would believe that Kati's mother could have lived at her parents' home with Kati and taken care of her as long as her health would allow. This behavior makes her seem as if she is an irrational mother.

Some readers might also look over the importance of the existence of the supernatural beings by thinking that Kati's mother is only afraid that she would hurt her daughter again and that is why she leaves Kati with her grandparents. However, the following statements show readers that because of her illness she had accidently hurt her daughter many times before but had not intended to leave Kati:

> You were hurt because of me many times—you got lumps on your head, a split lip. You used to cry so loudly when you were hurt too. But the next minute you would be playing happily as if nothing had ever happened.... But at this stage I became more and more certain that something was wrong with me. When I was finally diagnosed, I just couldn't think how I was going to manage my life at all. I took leave from work and went to live with Grandpa and Grandma. (p. 57)

Kati's mother making a wish and vow to give something in return is a normal practice in Thailand, though in her case it looks rather extreme. Such practice is popular in Thailand, a practice that has been integrated into the belief systems of Thais. Many Thais who practice Buddhism also have beliefs that supernatural things are able to fulfill wishes that they ask for.

Similar to other cultures, syncretism occurs in Thailand. That is, there is fusion of a variety of folk practices and different religions into the belief system of many Thais. For example, one of the most popular places in Thailand, even among Buddhists, involves making a wish at the Erawan shrine in Bangkok, a shrine devoted to a Hindu god. Flowers or fruit are offered when one makes a wish. When the wish is fulfilled, the wish maker has to give or do something in return as promised. Usually, people promise to hire Thai traditional dancers to perform where the shrine is located to please the god.

From a Thai perspective, Kati's mother is not perceived as an irrational mother who abandons her daughter because of her superstitious belief, but rather as a loving and dedicated mother who gives up the happiness of staying close to her child in exchange for her daughter's safety.

The portrayal of love as the self-sacrifice of parents can also be seen in some Thai novels. *Tricky Love* (Mingmitpattanakul, 2012) is an example. It is a novel written by *Kaotam* (เก้าแต้ม), a pen name. The novel became a popular TV series in 2016.

In the novel and TV series *Tricky Love*, the mother of the male leading character consults a fortune-teller about why her son has been injured in many accidents. The fortune-teller tells her that other spirits are jealous of her son because he has received good care from a kind mother, so they keep hurting him whenever they have a chance. If the mother still lives with him, he will die young. To stop them, the mother has to stay away from him until he turns twenty-eight.

This portrayal of love is not new. This kind of self-sacrifice of parents has been praised by Thai audiences for a long time.

Similar portrayals of the sacrifice of a mother or father who has to give up their children so the children would have a better life appear in other Thai novels, TV series, and plays, such as *For His Child* (Vajiravudh, 1981), which was written by His Majesty King Vajiravudh (1880–1925); *Aryarak* (Hiriotappa, 2000), a novel written with a pen name, *Jamlak* (จำลักษณ์) and made into a TV series in 1967, 1983, 2000, and 2013; and *Kue Huttha Krong Pipob* (Nawamanon, 1993), a novel written with a pen name *Nam-op* (น้ำอบ) and made into a TV series in 1995 and 2013.

The parents in those stories are not perceived as selfish or irrational because they abandon their children, but are considered devoted parents who love their children more than they love themselves. They do whatever it takes in exchange for their children's well-being.

KATI'S DECISION IN PURSUIT OF HAPPINESS

Before Kati's mother passes away, she leaves a letter for Kati that she wrote to her ex-husband. Kati must make the decision whether to send it to her father, a man she has never met. She eventually decides not to send the letter. The story does not tell readers why. Readers might question why Kati does not send the letter to her father. For example, one reviewer says:

> I think that, before she died, the mother should have talked to her about her father. It was unfair to the father and to Kati to not give her more complete background about the father. Sure, at 9 years old, she didn't feel the need to meet him, but what if she should change her mind? She has very little to go on to make that decision. (LauraW, 2011)

This type of comment exemplifies a misinterpretation of the story's most important message.

Kati grows up with her grandparents from her mother's side and always wonders about the absence of her mother, as seen from the title of the sub-headings of each chapter in the first part of the novel. However, readers as well as Kati know very little about Kati's father. As mentioned earlier, the novel does not explicitly tell why Kati's mother separated with her husband or whether he even knew that she was pregnant and gave birth to Kati. Uncle

Dong gives a hint about this matter when he shows Kati her mother's belongings at the apartment in the city after the funeral:

> Sometimes destiny plays such strange tricks on us humans, little Ti [Kati]. . . . It was in this very bag that your Mother carried with her all that she possessed on the day she decided to return to Thailand. Oh . . . all, that is, apart from you, the baby she was carrying in her womb. (Vejjajiva, 2006, p. 90)

The above statement suggests a sudden and sad departure. It is highly possible that her husband did not know that she was pregnant with Kati.

Kati also never asks about her father until she hears the story from Uncle Dong. Kati asks Aunt Da, who is her mother's close friend and colleague, about her father for the first time:

> "Did Mother hate Father?" Aunt Da was startled. She bent down to look at Kati's face and answered, "Your mother never spoke of your father to me and I never asked, because I only knew your mother afterwards. But I don't think your mother hated anyone. Especially anyone who helped her bring you into the world!" (p. 98)

Even after Kati learns that her mother might not hate her father, she decides not to send the letter to him. She could have asked more if she really wanted to know about her father.

Kati's decision not to send the letter to her father was not because she had never met him, but rather she is completely happy with her current life. In other words, she is filled with happiness. It is possible that because having the love of her mother's family and her mother's friends, Kati does not feel that she is missing something in her life, even her father. When she goes back to her grandparents' house in Ayutthaya, however, readers realize how content Kati is with her life: "Kati loved everything about this house. She was content with all she had here, and now there were no more lost or discarded pieces of her life to find" (p. 108).

Nobody really knows her decision. The people around her think she sends the letter. After many days, there is still no contact from Kati's father. Aunt Da is worried if Kati is sad. Uncle Dong says, "She probably will, but what can we do about it? . . . Kati is Pat's [Kati's mother] daughter. She is not as fragile as we all think, you know. She is really doing very well. She certainly has all our love" (p. 105).

The Happiness of Kati tells readers to appreciate what one has at the moment. "Happiness" in the author's view is not the happiness from fulfilling one's greed or chasing one's dreams but the happiness one finds in being content with and appreciative toward what one has in every step of his or her life.

Valuing happiness and appreciating one's current life is explicitly highlighted when Kati goes to the post office, and rather than sending a letter to her father she sends one to Tong, who is on a trip abroad:

> Gazing into the sky made you feel humble. It made your proudest ambitions dissolve into the ether, leaving only a little heart beating in a breast that tried its best to protect itself and find happiness where it could, not craving the impossible, not wanting things beyond its reach. (p. 105)

SUBTLETY OF HAPPINESS

Throughout the novel, the author privileges descriptive narratives over dialogues and subtlety over explicitness to imply Kati's state of being happy. "Happiness" could be a universal theme for many books around the world. In the novel, "Thai true happiness," or appreciation of a simple life, is effectively implied through the plain and simple country lifestyle Kati and her family members live.

The author particularly emphasizes a plain lifestyle through images of what a life in the country is like. These images represent the important elements of "happiness" Kati and other characters in the book embrace. For example, household goods, activities, school, and so on all represent the happiness of a simple and humble life that the author portrays.

Kati's school serves as one of the important aspects of her happiness. Kati is said to be educated in a local temple school. Readers from other cultures might assume that monks are the teachers in a temple school or have no idea what kind of school a temple school is. The author intentionally places Kati in a temple school in order to imply how simple and humble Kati's life is.

A temple school is a public school located in or near a temple. Although the school is called a temple school, monks are not involved in teaching. The curriculum follows the guideline by Thailand's Ministry of Education, and the grade-level structure is the same as other schools in Thailand.

Some temple schools in Thailand's capital, Bangkok, are big and well funded. However, many temple schools both in Bangkok and other provinces are small and not well funded. In other words, the quality of education at temple schools varies. Thai people usually associate a temple school with affordability but lower educational quality.

Initially, readers might assume that Kati is from a wealthy family because her grandparents and her mother were all educated abroad. Indeed, being educated overseas is an indication of wealth in a developing country like Thailand. However, Kati's life is described as humble, plain, and simple. Kati could have been sent to any highly regarded school in the province, but she appears to be educated in just a plain, local temple school where she does not need a lot of financial support. This point emerges later in the book where Kati's mother and her friend, Uncle Kunn, invested in developing a television show from overseas to support Kati's education:

> Tonight everyone at the table raised their glasses to celebrate with Kati, as the profit from the deal would go towards Kati's education. The grown-ups at the table roared with laughter when Kati, mystified, asked, "But I go to the local temple school, why do we need a lot of money for my education?" (p. 45)

The money from the investment that the grown-ups earned would not be spent on Kati's education at the local temple school. It means that they hopefully want to move Kati to a better school or spend money on furthering her education elsewhere. Nonetheless, the above scene shows Kati's satisfaction of a simple life at her school. Even though it is not a big or well-known school, she is still happy with it and does not see why she needs more money for her education.

Another example that reflects a simple life in a countryside is Kati's daily routine, which is described as having a slow pace of life. *The Happiness of Kati* begins with a scene of her daily routine. A part of her routine is to offer food to the monks with her grandfather. This practice is called *Sai Baat*, which means to fill up a monk's bowl. Although almsgiving, the giving of food or money to monks and the poor, was widely practiced and considered an act of virtue in England and other parts of Europe. Filling up the monk's bowl with food in the story is translated into English as "daily merit offering to the monk."

The offering to the monk is usually done every morning. The monks will walk to the residential area, or they will come by boat as they do at Kati's home by the canal. People who wish to offer food to the monks will prepare a variety of food and place it in containers or a plastic bag and wait for the monks to walk past their home or arrive at their pier. The translation describes it this way in the story: "A tray containing curry, vegetables and fried fish, each in a small, clean plastic bag, was beside him [Grandpa]" (p. 2).

In Thailand, cooked food is called *Gab-Khao*, which means something to eat with rice. Therefore, to make a perfect meal, you need some rice to eat with *Gab-Khao*. In the first chapter, readers learn, "With the addition of Kati's steaming bowl of rice, their daily merit offering to the monks was complete" (p. 2). The rice will be put in a small bowl, a portion enough for a monk, or in a big bowl and people scoop the rice out into the monk's food bowl.

Offering food to the monks is one of the ways to make a merit in Thailand. In Thai Buddhism, it is believed that offering food to the monks will bring you good blessings. Moreover, this good thing can be passed on to those who have passed away or given to those whom you did a wrong to in an earlier, past life, thus your wrongdoing is forgiven.

After the food is given, the monks will give you a blessing. To complete the practice, people usually pour water onto the ground, or into a container and then to the ground. As they pour the water, they will pray for anyone they want to pass the good blessing on to. This water-pouring practice is explained with an extended translation from the Thai version so readers of the English version will be able to picture what this practice looks like:

> Grandpa poured water from a little brass vessel onto the ground, completing the offering to the monks. Like a river flowing from the mountains to the sea, the water symbolised the merit they had earned and passed on to departed loved ones. Kati joined her prayers to Grandpa's and prayed silently that her own wishes would be granted. (p. 3)

This daily routine of preparing food, waiting for the monk who comes by a paddle boat, offering the food to the monk, and pouring water consumes a lot of time. This scene is not introduced only to tell readers about Kati's routine with her grandparents. It intends to illustrate that the characters appreciate the simple and slow pace of life in a countryside and that is the happiness they embrace.

The descriptions of the countryside and various Thai cultural references, in other words, are effectively used to imply that Kati and her family members are surrounded by their own happiness. Without understanding the important role the descriptions of the simple countryside plays in the novel, readers who are accustomed to direct and explicit descriptions may not be able to fully comprehend the novel's ultimate message: "happiness" is always within ourselves.

CONCLUSION

The decisions both Kati and her mother make in *The Happiness of Kati* are intimately related to subtle aspects of Thai culture that non-Thai readers may misinterpret or overlook. It is important to recognize that small details may actually have big impacts and are key parts of the story. These include Kati's mother, who holds on to her supernatural beliefs; Kati, who is happy and satisfied with her life in the country; and the images of a plain but happy country lifestyle portrayed through Thai cultural references.

All of these aspects of the novel represent significant parts of Thai culture, and the novel implies them with subtlety. Because some understanding of Thai culture is required for fuller comprehension, international readers may not fully understand the reasons why Kati and her mother made the decisions they did. They may not comprehend how the life in the countryside is intricately associated with the type of happiness Kati embraces.

It would be beneficial for international readers of these Thai stories to have some guidance about the cultural references made in *The Happiness of Kati* in order to more fully comprehend what they are reading and to gain a greater understanding of a people who are culturally different from themselves.

REFERENCES

Attanatho, P. (2010). In pursuit of Thainess in the English translation of *The Happiness of Kati*. *Journal of English Studies, 5*, 136–71.

Aungsuwan, W. (2007). The problems of non-equivalence at word level and translation strategies applied in the children's literature named *The Happiness of Kati* by Prudence Borthwick. *Journal of Language and Culture, 26*(1–2), 172–87.

Kriengkraipetch, S. (2000). Folksong and the socio-cultural change in village life. In S. Nathalang (Ed.), *Thai folklore insights into Thai culture* (pp. 143–68). Bangkok, Thailand: Chulalongkorn University Press.

LauraW. (2011). LauraW's reviews: *The happiness of Kati*. Retrieved from https://www.goodreads.com/review/show/141787139?book_show_action=true&from_review_page=1.

Mayosmith, I. (2006). Customer review. Retrieved from https://www.amazon.com/gp/customer-reviews/R3C0D7Q037SQQ1/ref=cm_cr_dp_d_rvw_ttl?ie=UTF8&ASIN=1741147530.

CHILDREN'S LITERATURE CITED

Vejjajiva, J. (2006). *The happiness of kati*. Translated by P. Borthwick. Bangkok, Thailand: Piggy Bank Press. เวชชาชีวะ, งามพรรณ. 2550. ความสุขของกะทิ. 34th ed. กรุงเทพฯ: แพรวสำนักพิมพ์.

NOVELS CITED

Hiriotappa, S. (2000). *Arya Ruk*. 2th ed. Bangkok, Thailand: Sanookarn. หิริโอตัปปะ, สำนาร์. (2543). อาญารัก. พิมพ์ครั้งที่ 2. กรุงเทพฯ: สนุกอ่าน.

Mingmitpattanakul, K. (2012). *Tricky Love*. Bangkok, Thailand: Pimkham. มิ่งมิตรพัฒนะกุล, คัคณางค์ (2555). กามเทพซ้อนกล. กรุงเทพฯ: พิมพ์คำ.

Nawamanon, E. (1993). *Kue Huttha Krong Pipob*. Bangkok, Thailand: Dokya. นวมานนท์, อิราวดี. (2536). คือหัตถาครองพิภพ. กรุงเทพฯ: ดอกหญ้า.

PLAY CITED

Vajiravudh, H. M. King. (1981). *For his child*. Bangkok, Thailand: Horatanachai Printing. พระมงกุฎเกล้าเจ้าอยู่หัว, พระบาทสมเด็จ (2524). เห็นแก่ลูก. กรุงเทพฯ: โรงพิมพ์หอรัตนชัย.

Chapter 3

Chinese Children Stories, Confucianism, and the Family

Haiyue (Fiona) Shan with Daniel Miles Amos

One of the difficulties readers who are not from East Asia may have in reading Chinese children's stories is the fact that these stories frequently have concepts found in Confucianism. Chinese readers influenced by Confucianism take for granted that stories are written from this perspective. However, those without this background may find it difficult to understand the hidden meaning behind Chinese children's stories. Using three stories read widely by Chinese children, this chapter delineates how Confucianism appears in these stories.

VALUES IN CONFUCIANISM

Chinese culture values the collectivist ideology of Confucianism, which ultimately affects the functions and behaviors of family and society (Yan & Sorenson, 2006). In China, Confucianism places emphasis on integration and cohesion, which is meant to promote stability and loyalty in the family, society, and country (Smolicz, Secombe, & Hudson, 2001). The interests and needs of the group supersede those of individuals.

Confucianism is a strongly patriarchal, hierarchical philosophy. Confucius (孔子, 551–479 BCE), the famed ancient political thinker, stated that there are five basic relationships: the emperor to subject, father to son, husband to wife, elder to younger, and friend to friend. That is, all relationships are based on social rank, gender, and age (all things being equal, men are superior to women, the younger person is lower than the elder; Tu, 1998). Although relations are now more relaxed and equal in Chinese society, Chinese parents still possess authority on big decisions, such as marriage, careers, and jobs (Huang & Gove, 2012).

The ideas of Confucius appear in Chinese children's stories, both past and present. Childhood is a critical period to develop cultural virtues, and values in China can be learned from traditional stories, folktales, and sayings.

The model of an ideal male in Confucianism is called *Junzi* (君子) in Chinese or a "noble person." To be a noble person in Confucianism does not necessarily mean that a man is an aristocrat but rather someone who has cultivated himself to the degree that he shows fine personal qualities and high moral principles. A noble person should possess five fundamental virtues: humanness, righteousness, ritual propriety, wisdom, and trustworthiness (Hird, 2017). Nobility is expressed in phrases such as "be sincere and not hypocritical," "treat others with honesty and respect," and "be large-minded, not petty."

Many stories deal with the "beautiful virtues" (美德) of Confucianism and suggest how they shape individual personality and character.

THE RELATIONSHIP OF THE HUSBAND TO THE WIFE

A key relationship within the family is that of the husband to the wife. The husband-wife relationship is essential for not only adding new family members but also for connecting two families that have been joined together by marriage (Sussman, 2013).

In the past, the duty of women in the extended family was to bear children in order to expand the family, to serve her husband and other family members, and to maintain harmony within the household. Women stereotypically assume the roles of wife and mother outside their native village. In the many areas of China where patrilocalism is practiced, new brides arrive as newcomers to live within their husband's family. Their fate is inevitably determined by the hierarchical position of their husband within his family, whether he is the eldest son or the middle or youngest son, and whether his family is impoverished or prosperous within the village or community (Chan, 2013; Huang & Gove, 2012).

Under no circumstances should women assume a dominating role. Within the tradition of Confucianism, this means that a daughter must listen to her father, as a wife she should follow her husband, and as a widowed mother she should obey her son (Tu, 1998).

The Chinese family system is characterized by the dominance of the father-son relationship (Hwang, 2000). Less attention is paid to the relation between husband and wife. In contrast, the importance of the husband-wife relationship in the United States is more prevalent and increasingly viewed as being horizontal, equal, voluntary, and breakable (Ho, 1998).

Chinese idioms about husband and wife reflect Confucian thought. They suggest that in the ideal husband-wife relationship, "The husband sings, the wife follows (夫唱妇随)," "Zither and flute are in harmony (琴瑟和鸣)," and "Treat one another with respect like honored guests (相敬如宾)." In summary, the couple should act in harmony, and this will be possible if the wife is following her husband's directions.

A widely known folktale from ancient China and still popular in modern times is *River Snail Girl* (田螺姑娘) (Ye, 2016), which was probably created around 380 CE and recorded in *A Postscript on the Search for Gods*《搜神后记》written by Tao Yuanming (陶渊明, 365?–427 CE), a great poet of the Six Dynasties period (317–479 CE).

One version of the story for children describes a young, hardworking, honest fisherman, an orphan from childhood, who lives alone. One day he finds a beautiful river snail away from water and cannot bear to let it die in the sun. He keeps it in a water jar, frequently changing the water. After keeping the river snail for several days, the fisherman returns home from a day of fishing and finds a delicious meal on his table and clean clothes on his bed. The fisherman asks his fellow villagers if they have helped him, but none answer in the affirmative.

One day the fisherman takes his nets to leave for fishing but comes right back and peeps inside his home. A lovely young girl emerges from the snail and begins preparing a sumptuous feast. The fisherman grabs her by her arm and asks who she is, and the girl says she is a fairy given by God to be his wife. Overjoyed, the fisherman lives happily with his fairy wife ever after. In contrast to many Chinese romances, this is a happy Chinese love story.

The story reflects the different roles of men and women and social division of labor in the Chinese family, where in theory men work outside the home and women stay inside the home and do housework, clean, and raise children (Giskin & Walsh, 2001). The idiom "Men exist on the outside, women on the inside (男主外, 女主内)" follows the Confucian assumption that "men and women are distinct (男女有别)." The image of women in this story is idealized; not only is the fairy wife sweet, gentle, and well behaved but she is also brave, kind, honest, and hardworking inside the home. These are all features that many Chinese men still dream about in a wife.

THE RELATIONSHIP OF THE YOUNGER TO THE ELDER

In collectivist societies like China, children grow up as members of their group and community and expect the group to protect them when they have needs or are in trouble. In return, children must remain loyal to their group

(Wong, 2001). In this tight-knit relationship, honor bestowed upon one member is shared by the entire group. Successful individuals can help other members of their group and frequently assist them in business affairs.

Since the Eastern Han dynasty (25–220 CE), Chinese parents have used the story *Kong Rong Shares the Pear* (Gang, 2015) to teach their children about humility and the importance of being considerate and caring toward siblings and friends.

The story focuses on Kong Rong, a four-year-old boy. One day, Kong Rong is asked by his father to distribute pears to his seven brothers. Kong Rong gives the bigger ones to his younger brother and six elder brothers and leaves himself with the smallest one. Watching Kong Rong's behavior, his father asks him why he acts in that way. Kong Rong answers that he wants to be humble. The Chinese admire the behavior of this innocent four-year-old boy who behaves so humbly and demonstrates filial piety.

Interestingly, when the same story was read to children in the United States they reacted differently from Chinese children. Children attending a Chinese language class in the United States had the following reactions to the story (刘, 2014):

- "Why does the behavior of keeping the smallest pear to himself represent a humble attitude to brothers?"
- "Didn't he basically show off how humble he was to his brothers?"
- "He could have shared the pears by cutting into pieces instead of taking the smallest one."
- "Why did Kong Rong believe that his older brothers would like to have the bigger pear?"
- "He may have not liked pears. Kong Rong should have asked his brothers their preferences first."
- "By giving others bigger pears, he showed his weakness in personality."

On the contrary, Chinese students praised Kong Rong for "being selfless and considerate to others," "respecting elders," and "being humble towards one's siblings" (刘, 2014). Most Chinese students would not question the motivations behind Kong Rong's behavior and the principles that guide him. The bigger pear in this story actually represents the greater interests of the family. Chinese readers admire the behavior of Kong Rong because he puts aside his own small interests in consideration of the large group, his brothers.

Some scholars have suggested that Westerners often adopt a more cognitive framework for analyzing the nature of humility (Kastanakis & Voyer, 2014; Wang & Chen, 2010). Americans, in particular, are more prone to emphasize the importance of equality rather than humility. They also tend to de-emphasize social hierarchy and differences in rank and status between people. The American child's statement that Kong Rong should have cut the pears into equal pieces especially reflects this line of thought.

Within Confucian traditions, humility in children emerges through behavior and action. Humility not only represents politeness but also is a display of virtue. Kong Rong represents the ideal that even a four-year-old child can comprehend his social standing and act with honor. Kong Rong sacrifices his desire to eat delicious pears, and thus supports his brothers' desires before his own. As a consequence, he has strengthened his bonds to his siblings and family.

Virtues and moral sensibilities do not come naturally in Confucianism but are gained through observation and lifelong learning. That is, one should make an effort to achieve a virtuous state by committing oneself to learning (Chien, Tai, & Yeh, 2012).

Within this same Confucian belief system, lifelong pursuit of perfection relies on the support of others, especially the support of family members who have an important role to play in promoting the education of children within their family and even within their larger clan group. Taking care of other family members is an essential responsibility, and the inability to keep one's family, lineage, and clan together by properly educating children is viewed as a profound failure (Zheng, 2016).

In contemporary China, many households still view education as a family business, and parents hold authority in making decisions about the education of their children (Huang & Gove, 2012). The outcome of children's education may bring shame or pride to the family. If children display high virtues or succeed in academics, it is a triumph of the entire family.

Therefore, it is no surprise that in the story *Kong Rong Shares the Pear* the little boy's father and brothers are proud of his behavior because Kong Rong's virtue reflects the contribution made by his parents and family members to his education. By choosing the smallest pear, Kong Rong demonstrates the positive outcome of his virtuous upbringing.

THE RELATIONSHIP BETWEEN FATHERS AND SONS

As mentioned above, the Chinese consider family to be the core element that holds society together (Slote & De Vos, 1998). In the Chinese family system as idealized by Confucianism, the patriarch, the father, is the interpreter, the executor, the standard holder of the moral code for all family members. A father must take responsibility to stabilize and maintain harmony among family members.

Over the past century and a half, especially since the encroachment of Western powers, in addition to Russia and Japan on China through colonialism, semicolonialism, and military invasion, China has undergone profound social changes that have altered the nature of the Chinese family (Chan, 2013; Chen, 2012). One tendency in the change from "traditional" to "modern" has been the growth of greater equality within the family structure (Chen & Chen, 2004).

A Chinese father-son relationship that is more "modern" but still Confucian is wonderfully described in the story *The Sight of Father's Back* (Zhu, 2012). The story has been used in Chinese middle school language classes for decades. It was originally published in 1925 by the well-known essayist Zhu Ziqing during a time of political turbulence and war in China.

The context of the story occurs when the author comes home to help his father with the funeral of his grandmother. The author needs to leave town immediately after the funeral. His father sends him off at the railroad station but is reluctant to part. He helps his son with his luggage and asks a man sitting in the tearoom to look after his son on the train. The father insists on walking to the train with his son and picks a seat for him closer to the exit. The father reminds his son to be alert during the nighttime and keep himself warm on the train.

At the end of the story, the father slowly limps toward a fruit shop to get his son oranges for his journey. The sight of his father's back makes a profound impression on his son.

Although the narrator of the story is already grown and has been away from his hometown for years, his father still attends to small things on his behalf. He feels the deep love of his father although the latter does not express his love explicitly and verbally.

In this story, it is obvious that both the father and the son recognize each other's love without openly uttering it. The father's familial role, his lifelong and implicit authority over his son, structurally distances him. Explicit expressions of deep feelings are intentionally avoided between the father and the son since the direct expression of emotion would indicate that they are weak and lack the emotional bearing and strength of males.

However, the bond of love between the father and the son in the story is clear throughout by the father's actions. The son reciprocates his father's love by letting his father attend to him. As the train departs, the son watches his father's tired and bent figure until he disappears from view.

CONCLUSION

Some studies describe the typical Chinese father as a stern disciplinarian, more concerned with the demand of propriety than with feelings, a man who is always feared by his children (Chan, 2013). Modern China is still influenced by Confucianism, but the father-son relationship has evolved into one of more equal status (Huang & Gove, 2012; Slote & De Vos, 1998). The forms of hierarchy inherited from former times have been transformed into ones of greater equality and mutual understanding between fathers and sons. The story *The Sight of Father's Back* beautifully shows the transformation from an older kind of Confucianism to a more contemporary version.

The same tendency toward greater equality has also emerged in other areas of contemporary Chinese social relationships, such as those between friends of different ages, between siblings, and between husbands and wives. Although a greater sense of equality now exists within the family, Confucian ideas are still readily used by Chinese people as a source of reference to explain and rationalize behavior within their families and friendships, and to explain social and political action within the larger society.

REFERENCES

Chan, S. T. (2013). East and West: Exploration of the father-son conflict in Chinese culture from the perspective of family triangulation in the West and the classical opera stories of the East. In K.-B. Chan (Ed.), *International handbook of Chinese families* (pp. 393–401). New York: Springer.

Chen, X. (2012). Human development in the context of social change: Introduction. *Child Development Perspectives, 6*(4), 321–25.

Chen, X.-P., & Chen, C. C. (2004). On the intricacies of the Chinese guanxi: A process model of guanxi development. *Asia Pacific Journal of Management, 21*(3), 305–24.

Chien, L.-Y., Tai, C.-J., & Yeh, M.-C. (2012). Domestic decision-making power, social support, and postpartum depression symptoms among immigrant and native women in Taiwan. *Nursing Research, 61*(2), 103–10.

Giskin, H., & Walsh, B. S. (2001). *An introduction to Chinese culture through the family.* Albany, NY: SUNY Press.

Hird, D. (2017). In league with gentlemen: Junzi masculinity and the Chinese nation in cultural nationalist discourses. *Asia Pacific Perspectives, 15*(1), 14–35.

Ho, D. Y. (1998). Interpersonal relationships and relationship dominance: An analysis based on methodological relationism. *Asian Journal of Social Psychology, 1*(1), 1–16.

Huang, G. H.-C., & Gove, M. (2012). Confucianism and Chinese families: Values and practices in education. *International Journal of Humanities and Social Science, 2*(3), 10–14.

Hwang, K. K. (2000). Chinese relationalism: Theoretical construction and methodological considerations. *Journal for the Theory of Social Behaviour, 30*(2), 155–78.

Kastanakis, M. N., & Voyer, B. G. (2014). The effect of culture on perception and cognition: A conceptual framework. *Journal of Business Research, 67*(4), 425–33.

Slote, W. H., & De Vos, G. A. (1998). *Confucianism and the family: A study of Indo-Tibetan scholasticism*. Albany, NY: SUNY Press.

Smolicz, J. J., Secombe, M. J., & Hudson, D. M. (2001). Family collectivism and minority languages as core values of culture among ethnic groups in Australia. *Journal of Multilingual and Multicultural Development, 22*(2), 152–72.

Sussman, N. M. (2013). Reforming family among remigrants: Hongkongers come home. In K.-B. Chan (Ed.), *International handbook of Chinese families* (pp. 53–76). New York: Springer.

Tu, W.-M. (1998). Probing the "three bonds" and "five relationships" in Confucian humanism. In W. H. Slote & G. A. De Vos (Eds.), *Confucianism and the family: A study of Indo-Tibetan scholasticism* (pp. 121–36). Albany, NY: SUNY Press.

Wang, G., & Chen, Y. (2010). Collectivism, relations, and Chinese communication. *Chinese Journal of Communication, 3*(1), 1–9.

Wong, Y. T. E. (2001). The Chinese at work: Collectivism or individualism? (HKIBS Working Paper Series 040-001). Retrieved from Lingnan University website: http://commons.ln.edu.hk/hkibswp/31.

Yan, J., & Sorenson, R. (2006). The effect of Confucian values on succession in family business. *Family Business Review, 19*(3), 235–50.

Zheng, R. (2016). The relationships between Confucian family values and attitudes toward divorce in mainland China: An exploratory study. *Dissertations—ALL*. 611. http://surface.syr.edu/etd/611.

(IN CHINESE)

刘桂萍. (2014). 中美学生批判性思维能力的差异给我们的启示——以《孔融让梨》的解读为例. *中学语文教学, 12*, 16–18.

CHILDREN'S LITERATURE CITED

Gang, X. (2015). *Kong Rong shares the pear* (in Chinese). ChangChun, China: Jilin Fine Arts Publishing House.

Ye, C. (2016). *River snail girl*. Beijing, China: Sinolingua.

Zhu, Z.-Q. (2012). *The sight of father's back* (in Chinese). Anhui, China: Anhui Peoples Publishing House.

Chapter 4

The Monkey within You

Journey to the West, *an Essential Text of Chinese Religion and Folk Cosmology*

Daniel Miles Amos

I lived in mainland China in 1980, and during my lunch hour I listened to all one hundred chapters of *The Journey to the West* as they were performed on the radio by a single, wonderfully gifted storyteller. At the beginning of the twentieth century approximately 90 percent of Chinese were unable to read (Ross, 2005), and even by 1980 nearly 40 percent of China's population was illiterate (Zhang, 2006).

One consequence of large-scale illiteracy has been that throughout China's history itinerant storytellers provided entertainment to a vast, unlettered population, orally retelling tales and works of literature. All of China's popularly recognized four literary masterpieces from the Ming (明朝; 1368–1644) and Qing dynasties (清朝; 1644–1911)—*Water Margin* (水滸傳), *Romance of the Three Kingdoms* (三國演義), *Dream of the Red Chamber* (紅樓夢), and *The Journey to the West* (西遊記)—are written in formats that are friendly to oral performance.

For example, to encourage the unlettered rural and urban listeners to return the next day to their performances of *The Journey to the West*, itinerant storytellers made use of the novel's cliffhangers that end every chapter but the last one. The following is a typical chapter ending, in which the Heavenly preceptor describes the capture of Monkey King, and the ruler of Heaven, the Jade Emperor, orders Monkey to be cut to pieces:

"The Four Great Devarajas have captured the monstrous monkey, the Great Sage, Equal to Heaven. They await the command of Your Majesty." The Jade Emperor then gave the order that the demon king Mahalbali and the heavenly guardians take the prisoner to the monster execution block, where he was to be cut to small pieces.... We do not know what will become of the Monkey King, and you must listen to the explanation in the next chapter. (Yu, 1977, p. 165)

The brief paragraph above makes many religious references, and Monkey King has penetrated into many Chinese people's ways of believing, thinking, and behaving. This chapter analyzes the meaning and religious significance of *The Journey to the West* for Chinese culture. In addition to giving a synopsis of the novel and its characters, Chinese folk religion is outlined in the briefest of terms.

In more detail, examples are provided of how the novel itself has supported the development of Chinese folk religion over time, and it currently functions as part of the belief systems of many Chinese, including some populations within mainland China and segments of the population in Hong Kong, Macau, Taiwan, and among overseas Chinese. A brief background exposition about the version of Chinese folk religion presented in the novel is necessary for readers who lack this knowledge and is essential for beginning even the briefest journey into the work.

CHINESE FOLK RELIGION AS EXPRESSED IN THE NOVEL

Gods, ghosts, and ancestors (神, 鬼, 祖先) are worshipped in Chinese folk religion (Jordan, 2012). Numerous gods and spirits exist, and they are hierarchically ranked and stratified into classes from most to least powerful, like people in Chinese society and all state-level societies.

A central character in *The Journey to the West* is the Great Benevolent Sage of Heaven, the Celestial Jade Emperor (玉帝), who, attended by his divine ministers, sits in the Cloud Palace of the Golden Arches. In popular Chinese religion the Jade Emperor is one of the representations of the first God; in Daoism (道教) he is one of the primordial emanations, signifying living in harmony with "the way" (道).

The Jade Emperor is the chief Heavenly Deity, ruler of all other gods and immortal spirits in Heaven who attend to Heavenly bureaucratic offices, and he rewards and punishes them according to their merit. The Jade Emperor can be thought of as a Heavenly equivalent of the idealized, omnipotent emperors of China's past who were thought to rule all people who populate the earth.

The highest god in Heaven in *The Journey to the West*, however, is a Deity from another spiritual realm, and is more powerful than the Jade Emperor. When Monkey King became dissatisfied with the lowly position that the Jade Emperor has assigned him in Heaven, he rebelled. He stole and ate peaches from the Garden of Immortal Peaches; he took the elixir of Laozi (老子,

the founder of Daoism), left the Celestial Palace, and attempted to seize the Heavenly throne.

Not one hundred thousand of the Jade Emperor's troops could subdue him, not the greatest of the divine Buddhist warriors, and not the immortal Thirty-Six Thunder Generals. Against the dire threat posed by Monkey King, the Jade Emperor panicked and sent an urgent request for assistance from a deity even more powerful than himself, Buddha (佛).

Not all types of Buddhism treat Buddha as a god. Followers of many versions of Zen (禪), for example, treat Buddha as a human being, Gautama Siddhartha, a prince born in the mountains of what in now Nepal, who lived in the sixth and fifth centuries BCE and during the course of his life discovered the true path to enlightenment. In Chinese folk religion, Buddha is the founding deity and head of his own alternative celestial paradise, composed of Buddhist gods and saints who are hierarchically ranked under him, similar to the stratification of the gods and spirits in the Heaven ruled by the Jade Emperor.

Guan Yin (觀音, commonly called the Goddess of Mercy in English) is one of the most important Buddhist deities, and temples in her honor are found throughout Southeast Asia and East Asia. In *The Journey to the West* Guan Yin is Buddha's most important assistant and collaborator. It is Guan Yin who recruits the pilgrims, and like a good fairy in a European fairy tale, she sometimes aids them when they are unable to overcome the forces against them. Significantly, Guan Yin has devised a magical instrument that can control the unruly Monkey King, having placed a golden ring around his head that causes him agony when either she or Tripitaka (the monk selected by Guan Yin to bring back the Buddhist texts from India) chants the mantra that tightens the ring around Monkey's head.

Laozi, whose name literally means "Old Guy" in Chinese, was the ancient Chinese philosopher who is reputed to have written the *Dao De Jing* (道德經) and to have founded Daoism (道教). He is a deity in both religious Daoism and Chinese folk religion. In *The Journey to the West*, Laozi is an important deity in the Heaven ruled by the Jade Emperor, but an ineffectual and humorous one, completely unable to control Monkey King. In Chinese history Daoism has at times been in fierce competition with Buddhism, and in *The Journey to the West*, a novel that celebrates Buddhism, Daoist monks appear as the villains of many chapters.

It has been asserted that Chinese fiction developed during a period between the Yuan and Ming dynasties (1277–1644) when there was a creative sociocultural fusion between the folk art of storytellers, combined with bits of history and borrowed literary fragments (Fu, 1977). It was through storytellers that knowledge of the great Chinese novels spread throughout the population, and the fictional depictions of the personalities and events of the characters in the novels became incorporated into Chinese folk culture, religion, and popular cosmology.

For example, Guan Yu (關羽) was a Chinese historical figure, a leading general during the late Eastern Han (東漢; 25–220 CE) under the warlord Liu Bei (劉備; 161–223 CE). After Guan Yu's execution in 220 CE, he was held to be the personification of loyalty and martial virtue. By the early Sui dynasty (隋朝; 581–618) Guan Yu had been deified (Roberts, 2014) and had become the Chinese equivalent of the God of War.

Guan Yu is revered throughout East Asia, and in Chinese culture he is worshipped in popular Confucianism, Chinese Buddhism, Daoism, and Chinese folk religion. However, popular understanding of Guan Yu's life and character is not based on historical studies but on fiction, namely the classic Chinese novel *Romance of the Three Kingdoms* written during the early Ming dynasty. The god Guan Yu has a central place in Chinese folk religion and is admired by people from widely different social spheres and professions. In Hong Kong, for example, he is worshipped by policemen, while members of criminal gangs (黑社會) also pray to him (Amos, 2016).

In regard to the development of Chinese folk religion, it has been noted that most of the gods in popular Chinese religion are spirits of former human beings who have been deified, and "since these gods were once human, they understand the needs of their worshippers, and furthermore they need their offerings and recognition if they are to keep their position as gods" (Overmyer, 1998, pp. 51–52).

Like Guan Yu, Monkey King is also a god in Chinese folk religion, but contrary to most gods he originated not as a historical human being but as a mythological character. His powers, weaknesses, temptations, crimes, and strengths have also been defined and closely elaborated by the literary art of the one-hundred-chapter version of *The Journey to the West*. Similar to the cultural dynamics that created the details of Guan Yu's personality and life history in folk culture, the telling of the novel *The Journey to the West* by generations of itinerant storytellers brought Monkey King (also known as Sun Wukong孫悟空) to life as a powerful, mischievous deity in the minds of China's unlettered rural and urban folk.

It has been observed that *The Journey to the West* has many parallels to the third-century BCE epic Indian poem *Ramayana*, traditionally ascribed to the Hindu sage Valmiki (Walker, 1998). The *Ramayana* epic has Hanuman, a monkey-hero general as a main character, and it has been argued that the Chinese author of *The Journey to the West* borrowed from the much earlier work in his characterization of the Monkey King.

The *Ramayana* epic is "not just a story or legend but a religious text for Hinduism, comparable to the Koran or Torah" (Walker, 1998, p. 32). It is not an exaggeration to assert the same for *The Journey to the West*, which provides spiritual authority—a testament and covenant for followers of Chinese folk religion, clearly describing and defining the spiritual roles of Buddha, Buddhist gods and saints, together with the Heaven of many Deities ruled by the Jade Emperor.

ORIGIN AND EVOLUTION OF THE NOVEL

A kernel of history serves as the starting point for *The Journey to the West*, one of China's most important novels. Xuanzang (玄奘; 596–664), also known by the honorific Tripitaka (a traditional term for Buddhist scriptures), was a late Sui dynasty (隋朝; 581–618), early Tang dynasty (唐朝; 618–907) Buddhist monk who was dissatisfied with the limited quantity and poor quality of translations of Buddhist scriptures in China (Yu, 1977).

In defiance of Emperor Taizong's (太宗; 598–649) ban on travel, in 629 Tripitaka left Chang'an (長安, present-day Xian西安), the imperial capital, and began a journey to the west to India, where he hoped to gather Buddhist texts and study how to translate them. Defying Taizong, one of China's great emperors and cofounder of the Tang dynasty with his father, was a courageous act. Tripitaka's travels to and from India, his studies of Buddhism there and in Buddhist temples along the way, took seventeen years. When he returned to Chang'an in 646 bearing Buddhist texts, Emperor Taizong personally welcomed him (Yu, 1977).

During the Song dynasty (宋朝; 960–1279), a somewhat primitive poetic tale of Tripitaka's journey to the west was published. Its most significant aspect was the introduction of a companion, protector, and guide to Tripitaka, a Monkey novice-monk who by the conclusion of the poem had earned the title Great Sage (大聖) (Dudbridge, 1970).

A far more accomplished version of the journey to the west tale of Tripitaka, his monkey-hero companion, and other companions as well was published in Nanjing (南京), possibly in 1592 (Dudbridge, 1970). Renowned scholar and diplomat Hu Shih (胡適; 1891–1962) attributes this version to Wu Cheng-en (吳承恩; 1501–82), a provincial poet, scholar, and minor government official. However, *The Journey to the West* was published anonymously, and there is not universal agreement on its authorship (Lattimore, 1983).

Throughout Asia representations of monkey-heroes "are depicted in oral narration, theater, art, and, in modern times, and television shows. Shrines have been erected by devoted worshippers to pay homage to them. Clearly, the popularity of these monkey heroes is without question" (Walker, 1998, p. 8).

The Indian *Ramayana* monkey-hero stories, combined with Chinese folktales about monkeys beginning as early as China's Chu kingdom

(楚國; 704–223 BCE), in addition to more recent Chinese monkey-hero tales in many areas of China, especially places that had contact with Arab and Indian traders, such as port cities like Quanzhou, Fujian Province (福建泉州), provided rich foreign and indigenous Chinese cultural background for an author during the late Ming dynasty to create *The Journey to the West* (Walker, 1998).

SYNOPSIS OF THE NOVEL

In the Song dynasty poem about Tripitaka's journey to India, the mischievous monkey is a secondary, supporting character. By the time the one-hundred-chapter masterpiece *The Journey to the West* was published during the late Ming dynasty, Sun Wukong (孫悟空), or Monkey King, Great Sage, Equal to Heaven (齊天大聖), had become the central character of the work. One would suspect that Monkey became the dominant character in the novel because he is a trickster hero, a genius at angering and unsettling powerful authorities, both Heavenly and earthbound, and for this reason is loved everywhere.

The late Anthony C. Yu, who masterfully translated all one hundred chapters of *The Journey to the West* into English, wrote that the novel can be divided into five sections:

(Chapters 1–7): An immortal stone gave birth to an egg, which when exposed to wind transformed into a monkey. Monkey gained immortality and magical powers, and during his invasion of Heaven he single-handedly fought all the gods of Heaven and was almost victorious, causing great chaos, only to be easily defeated, subjugated, and imprisoned for centuries under a mountain by Buddha.

(Chapter 8): Buddha makes the decision to provide Buddhist canon to the Chinese people. He assigns Guan Yin the task of finding a virtuous man, such as Tripitaka, to serve as the pilgrim for the risky and arduous journey to the Indian continent, where Buddhism originated and developed.

Along the way Guan Yin recruits a band of misfits who have all been convicted of crimes by the Jade Emperor. More violent and powerful than the criminals recruited for the suicide mission in the US war film *The Dirty Dozen*, a band of frightening, convicted spirits will accompany Tripitaka on the pilgrimage, and they will have the possibility of changing their sentences and earning merit in Heaven by facing great peril to protect him. The monstrous misfits are recruited by Guan Yin in the order that follows below.

Sha Wujing (沙悟淨), Sandy, the former Curtain-Raising Marshal under the Jade Emperor in Heaven, clumsily broke a priceless crystal cup. In punishment, the Jade Emperor changed him into a river ogre who inhabits the

Flowing Sand River. Driven by hunger, every few days he leaves the river and devours people, including Buddhist pilgrims.

Zhu Bajie (豬八戒), Pig, Piggy, Monk Pig, Idiot, is a foolish pig demon consumed with lust and gluttony. Formerly, he was the Marshal of the Heavenly Reeds of the Heavenly River but got drunk and dallied with the Goddess of the Moon. For these crimes the Jade Emperor had him beaten two thousand times with a mallet and changed him into a pig-man fiend. After his punishment and transformation, Piggy satisfied his hunger by eating people, also including Buddhist pilgrims in his diet.

Bai Longma (白龍馬), the White Dragon Horse, a young dragon, third son of the Dragon King of the Western Ocean, inadvertently set fire to his father's palace and destroyed magical pearls within given to his father by the Jade Emperor. Punished with three hundred lashes and sentenced to death, he is saved from execution by Guan Yin, who intercedes on his behalf, telling the Jade Emperor that the White Horse Dragon will serve as the mount for Tripitaka during his hazardous journey to the west.

Sun Wukong, Monkey King, Monkey, Handsome Monkey King, Ape, the most powerful, brightest, mischievous, playful, and dangerous member of the gang, formerly enjoyed the taste of human flesh, too, luring travelers into his cave by transforming himself into a beautiful woman and capturing and eating his victims as he pleased, steamed or boiled.

When Guan Yin appeared Monkey promised her that his imprisonment of five hundred years under a mountain had taught him the meaning of penitence. Monkey King next said the words that lead Guan Yin to free him and make him one of the pilgrims to accompany and protect Tripitaka: "I entreat the Great Compassion to show me the proper path, for I am willing to practice religion" (Yu, 1977, p. 195).

(Chapters 9–12): These chapters provide details of Tripitaka's birth and family background, the journey of the great Emperor Taizong through the underworld, holding mass for the dead, and Guan Yin's realization that Tripitaka should receive the sacred commission for the pilgrimage to the west.

(Chapters 13–97): These chapters make up the main body of the work and describe the eighty-one ordeals suffered by the five pilgrims and their capture and escape from monsters, demons, gods, and others during their pilgrimage to and from India.

(Chapters 98–100): These chapters describe the successful return of the five pilgrims to Chang'an, capital of the Tang dynasty. All receive honors from Emperor Taizong for bringing back Buddhist scriptures to China.

Next, they are whisked away to Spirit Mountain, where all five appear before Buddha and are canonized in descending order of holiness (Yu, 1977). Tripitaka is promoted to the highest position of the five, Buddha of Candana Merit. In the sense understood by followers of Chinese folk religion,

Tripitaka became a Buddha because he had attained complete enlightenment and thus became an eternal Buddhist deity under the first and primary deity, Buddha.

Also canonized as a Buddha in the novel but one step lower than Tripitaka, Monkey King became a deity as well. Because of the virtue he gained in protecting Tripitaka, his devotion to Buddhism after his conversion, and his wonderful martial ability used in defense of Tripitaka and his mission, Monkey was named Buddha Victorious in Strife, the lowest ranking of all the Buddha divinities listed in the text and the only Buddha born in the shape of an animal.

Even after the pilgrimage has been successfully completed, Piggy retained an enormous appetite and remained far too talkative for his own good. He complained to Buddha that it was unfair he had not been deemed a Buddha in the manner of Tripitaka and Monkey King but made only a Bodhisattva (a divine saint and hero of Buddhism) and had been given the lowly task of serving as Janitor of the Buddhist Altars.

Buddha explained that this truly was not a bad position given the state of Piggy's vast appetites, implying that he had been appointed Janitor of the Altars because it gave him the opportunity to clean up after every Buddhist service, when there would always be plenty of delicious food remaining at the altars for him to eat after every service.

Of the final two pilgrims, Sandy became Bodhisattva, Golden-Bodied Arhat of Eight Jewels, the second lowest ranking Bodhisattva; while the White Dragon Horse became the Bodhisattva of Vast Strength, the Heavenly Dragon of Eight Divisions of Supernatural Beings, the lowest ranking and only Bodhisattva of nonhuman origins listed in the novel.

MONKEY KING AND THE LIVES OF ORDINARY CHINESE

Characters from the novel, such as Monkey King and Piggy, are popular deities who can be called to intervene and aid in the lives of ordinary Chinese people and are found in many spheres of life, some of which are discussed below.

Monkey King Temples, Festivals, and Cantonese Opera

Temples are dedicated to the Monkey King throughout greater China; for example, the Monkey King Temple (literally, the "Treasure Temple of the Great Sage" 大聖寶廟) located next to the Po Tat Estate in Sau Mau Ping, Kowloon, Hong Kong (九龍秀茂坪寶琳路寶達邨猴王廟), where he is worshipped as the principal god, together with lesser gods, such as his travel companions from the novel.

The current one-story Monkey King Temple was built in 2013. It is located next to the two-story Tin Hau Temple, which was built in 2012. Tin Hau, 天后, Empress of Heaven, originally protector of seafarers, is one of the most popular gods in Chinese folk religion, there being more than one hundred Tin Hau Temples in Hong Kong alone. A City God Temple (城隍廟) and a Guan Yin Temple (觀音廟), also one of the most numerous temples, are nearby.

Figure 4.1 Entrance to the Monkey King Temple (literally translated: Treasure Temple of the Great Sage), Sau Mau Ping, Kowloon, Hong Kong.

Figure 4.2 Bas-Relief Monkey King on the Monkey King Temple.

All four temples were originally located at a site near their present location. They were demolished in 2008 (Billinge, 2018) to make room for the forty-five-story high rise apartments of the Po Tat Estate (寶達邨) that now tower over them.

The Monkey King Temple is staffed by an elderly spirit medium, whose actions are guided by the Monkey King. The spirit medium and his family live in a modest home adjoining the temple. (In contrast, the Tin Hau Temple is not staffed by religious specialists such as Buddhist monks and nuns and was built by a seventy-nine-year-old local woman, who raised money to support its construction and lives inside the temple with other elderly women.)

In Hong Kong, temple festivals are held in honor of deities such as Monkey King, who have temples dedicated to them, and Monkey King's festival, like those of most other gods, occurs on the occasion of his "birthday." The Monkey King Festival (齊天大聖千秋) is held during the sixteenth day of the eighth month of the lunar calendar (falling in September according to the Common Era calendar), following the Mid-Autumn Festival by one day.

During the Monkey King Festival, the spirit medium, currently in his eighties, becomes possessed by Monkey King, and re-enacts Monkey's ferocious battles with other Heavenly gods and demons. Having become Monkey, the spirit medium is invincible, acquiring eyes of diamonds and other impenetrable body parts. When the spirit medium was still in his seventies, he would run barefoot across a bed of hot coals, climb a ladder made of seventy-two sharp knives, wash his face in boiling oil, chew glass, and cut his tongue with a sword, but he no longer performs these feats.

About two weeks before the date of Monkey King's birthday, mat-shed builders arrive and begin putting up a temporary bamboo and tin sheet Cantonese opera stage. The Monkey King Temple in Hong Kong is not fully covered by a roof, similar to temples dedicated to other gods, so that Monkey King can see the operas that are being performed in his honor.

Because operatic performances on these occasions are dedicated to temple gods, they are imbued with ritual and spiritualism, and "both actors and audience are always aware that another 'chief spectator' is mystically present, a knowledge that can presumably add one more dimension to the total experience of watching and performing traditional operas on the occasion of a temple festival" (Ward, 1979, p. 9).

Many regional and traditional operas (戲曲) exist in Chinese culture, including one of the oldest forms, Kunqu (崑曲), in addition to Shaoxing opera (紹興戲曲), Beijing opera (京劇), Cantonese opera (粵劇), and others. Operas about *The Journey to the West* and Monkey King occur in many of the Chinese operatic forms.

For instance, *True and False Handsome Monkey King* (真假美猴王), a Cantonese opera about Monkey King and the other pilgrims, is inspired by chapters 57 and 58 of the novel. In the opera, a six-ear macaque shapeshifts and becomes an exact copy of Monkey King, along with other monkeys who have shapeshifted down to the smallest hair into identical copies of the other pilgrims. Collectively, the shapeshifters challenge the sacred mission of the pilgrims, resulting in a ferocious battle between Monkey King and his false doppelganger, causing disturbance throughout the cosmos.

Another popular Cantonese opera is *Monkey King Fights White-Bone Lady Three Times* (孙悟空三打白骨精), inspired by chapter 27 of the novel. This opera also includes a shapeshifter as the prime antagonist, the White-Bone Lady, who desires to kill and eat the flesh of Tripitaka.

The White-Bone Lady appears before the pilgrims three times: first, as a beautiful girl "with a face like the moon and features like flowers" (Yu, 1978, p. 19), and tries to offer the travelers poisoned food. Monkey attacks her and seems to kill the young woman, to the horror of his companions; but the White-Bone Lady is not finished.

She next appears as an elderly woman, pretending to be the girl's mother; and finally, as an elderly man pretending that his daughter and wife are missing. Only Monkey King has the ability to perceive that it is the White-Bone Lady who has appeared before them on all three occasions. He attacks the shapeshifted female demon each time before finally finishing her off. Unfortunately, Monkey King's traveling companions are convinced that he has murdered a beautiful and innocent young woman and her family, and they temporarily expel him from their group.

The spirit medium and his family, who serve as the Monkey King Temple caretakers, speak with obvious pride about the Monkey King Festival and the large crowds of temple supporters who arrive to sustain Monkey King. During this time the audience bears witness to Monkey's physical reappearance when his spirit possesses the spirit medium, and on the days honoring his birth many can feel Monkey's presence during the Cantonese operas performed in his honor.

Monkey King and Shen Da Martial Arts

Another sphere of Chinese culture that makes spiritual use of Monkey King, Piggy, and other characters from the novel is a form of Chinese martial arts practiced in Hong Kong called Shen Da (神打). Shen Da involves spirit possession, and Monkey King, Piggy, and other gods from the novel frequently inhabit its practitioners. The most active and numerous practitioners of Shen Da in Hong Kong are adolescent males and young men, although females sometimes also practice the art.

Affective brotherhoods become Shen Da sworn brotherhoods when one sworn brother who is a Shen Da expert convinces his "brothers" to follow his teachings.

When new followers decide to practice Shen Da, they are initiated in a ceremony that involves striking them with a sharp object. The Shen Da master lines up the newcomers and prepares to hack their bare bellies with a sword or meat cleaver. Some Shen Da practitioners say that the sword should be as sharp as a razor because the sharper the sword the less pain. The master, who is possessed by a powerful god, such as Piggy or Monkey King, speaks magical words to report to the ancestral master that the initiates desire to join his "family" and tells him that the initiates are not afraid to be struck. The initiates are not possessed by spirits at this time.

After the master has made his report to the ancestor master, he strikes each initiate on the belly with a sword or cleaver. One respondent said that being struck by the sword feels like a person's hand does when it slaps a ball and is painful, like being stung by ants. Ideally, according to some Shen Da practitioners, after each initiate is struck with the sword or cleaver there should only be a little blood, so that it does not flow out but just oozes a little. Not to bleed at all may not be the best sign, and it is a bad sign to bleed heavily.

Some of the author's long-time "brothers" in a Hong Kong Praying Mantis martial arts brotherhood also practice Shen Da boxing and follow a Shen Da master in another brotherhood. When I first met their shirtless, obese middle-aged Shen Da master, the first thought that came into my mind was that he looked like Zhu Bajie (Piggy).

After witnessing the master's son and several of his brothers practicing Shen Da and being struck on the abdomen with a large, heavy meat cleaver, the master invited me to practice Shen Da. When I declined, stating that I do not know the art and do not know how to be possessed by a god, I was told not to worry. It was not necessary for me to be possessed by a god because the Shen Da master's god (who really was Piggy) would protect me. I declined once again, but when a few of my "brothers" pushed and pulled me into place for the ceremony, I took off my shirt and prepared for my demise.

The master struck me heavily three times on the belly with the meat cleaver. The blows were painful, but the sawing motions of the cleaver across my belly were more alarming. No blood flowed from my body that night, but when I awoke the next morning my abdomen was sore and there was a large green bruise across the width of my belly.

To become possessed by a powerful god such as Monkey King or Piggy, the neophyte Shen Da learner, similar to a neophyte marijuana smoker (Becker, 2015), must learn to recognize the signs of his transformation. A neophyte Shen Da boxer must learn to harmonize his actions with those of the god that possesses him, but many beginners are luan tong (亂通) because there is no coordination between the god and them. The Shen Da boxer might want to strike upward with his fist while doing a set of Kung Fu, but the force of the spirit might stop him or force him to strike downward. The Shen Da boxer must practice in order to unite with the deity.

Sometimes boxers do not know which god has descended upon them, although experienced Shen Da boxers can nearly always tell. Even if a Shen Da boxer knows which god has possessed him, his "brothers" may not be allowed to ask which one it is because the question would be disrespectful to the god. If a Shen Da boxer sincerely wishes for a particular god such as Monkey King, he may not necessarily be favored by the visitation, but a variation such as the Golden-Haired Monkey may come instead.

An initiated boxer can be positive, however, that if he asks for the Monkey King a completely different kind of god, such as Piggy, will not come instead. A study participant who is frequently possessed by Monkey King exclaimed, "You can feel the Monkey within you!"

Another Shen Da boxer described his first failed attempt at Shen Da possession in the following way:

> It was very strange. For the first night a god did not visit me, although I tried very hard and although my master helped me. We each held a stick of incense with our palms close together to await the descent of the spirits. During the first night there was no sign of a deity before the stick of incense burnt out.

The next time the same young man attempted to practice Shen Da and become possessed by a spirit he was successful. Rather than stand and try to become possessed, he decided to sit in a lotus position. Soon the deity arrived within him:

> I felt very elated when the deity descended on me. I'd never felt like that before. Originally, my palms were held fixed in front of me. Then suddenly, they began to move up and down, as in worshipping. I couldn't stop the worshipping motion of my hands. It became so funny that I laughed. Usually my breathing becomes very fast when I am possessed. That's what happened that night. I remember the first time even my face got numb. It was as if some external sucking force was pulling at my skin and causing it to swell.

An expert Shen Da boxer, one strong enough to be effectively possessed by Monkey King, may partly close his eyes and be able to see Hell, wandering souls, and unclaimed spirits. In emergency situations such as fights, initiated Shen Da boxers of any level of experience are able to immediately call for a spirit.

Needless to say, many middle-class Hong Kong Chinese are suspicious of Shen Da, believing that most of its practitioners are delinquents or gang members. At the same time, some of these same middle-class Chinese respect the powers of Shan Da boxers and do not belittle their supernatural abilities.

VERSIONS OF *THE JOURNEY TO THE WEST* FOR READERS AT DIFFERENT LEVELS

Only forty pages long, elementary school children would enjoy the version of Monkey King created by the acclaimed Chinese American artist and author

Ed Young (2001). Young, whose Mandarin Chinese name is Yang Zhicheng (杨志成), was born in Tianjin (天津), China, and since childhood he has had a strong connection to the Monkey King stories.

There are many versions of Monkey King available for young readers, but Caldecott Medal winner Ed Young's book has beautifully simple, meaningful phrasing that is offset by gorgeous and culturally informed collages. The book is comprehensible to young readers and a sumptuous treat for everyone.

A book that middle school students may enjoy reading is Arthur Waley's (1943) abbreviated translation of *The Journey to the West* that he called *Monkey, Folk Novel of China*. Waley's translation is less challenging, not one-third the length of the Chinese original now fully translated into English. When Waley's *Monkey* appeared during World War II it was considered to be superior in style to all other translations of *The Journey to the West*.

This remained true until 1983 when the final volume of Anthony C. Yu's superb four-volume translation of the Chinese masterpiece was published in English. While praising Waley's talents as a translator, Professor Yu (1977) was disappointed that Waley (1943) had translated so little of the novel, and dismayed that so few of the 750 poems that are critical to the story's narration appear in his predecessor's translation: "Not only is the fundamental literary form of the work thereby distorted, but also much of the narrative vigor and descriptive power of its language which have attracted so many generations of Chinese readers is lost" (Yu, 1977, p. x).

When reviewing the four volumes (1977, 1978, 1980, and 1983) of Yu's translation of *The Journey to the West*, one professor of Chinese literature suggested, "If you know a 12-year-old, give him or her the 'Monkey' of Arthur Waley. Do not be surprised, though, if your 12-year-old comes back for more—for the whole thing, Mr. Yu's *Journey to the West*" (Lattimore, 1983, para. 18).

Another way for students to gain insight from the novel is by preparing for and performing one of the English language plays inspired by *The Journey to the West*. A single Chinese operatic production can take days of acting and singing to perform. In contrast, English language plays based on *The Journey to the West* are by nature brief and attenuated but have the potential to be a valuable learning experience for high school and college students who are part of the production.

For example, *The Tale of Monkey: His Magic Journey to the West*, written by Australian playwright Bryan Nason (2003), is a play that can be performed by high school and university students. For one who knows the novel, watching the play is like "viewing flowers from horseback" (走馬觀花)—in other words, superficial compared to the book. Naturally, because the play is brief and tries to pack in one hundred chapters into a compact story of 120 minutes, by nature and circumstance it loses context and much of the vast richness of the original novel.

Nevertheless, when performed well the play is entertaining, and student performances can be impressive and provide evidence of cross-cultural learning. Part of the learning students should experience is a greater understanding of the role of white supremacy and racism when depicting Asians in works of art in the United States. When casting for the play, it should be essential for students and faculty members to have a collective discussion of "whitewashing." This is especially important as Hollywood has a long history of whitewashing and is still frequently guilty of the practice.

Recent films such as *Ghost in the Shell* starring Scarlett Johansson, *The Great Wall* starring Matt Damon, and *Doctor Strange* starring Tilda Swinton are reprehensible in their use of white actors for Asian characters, still all too common in an era when a white actor appearing in blackface is completely taboo. Hollywood's racist depictions of Asians and use of white actors in Asian roles is especially culpable since the industry has vast resources and a large pool of talented Asian and Asian American actors to choose from.

It can be noted, however, that most of the central characters in *The Journey to the West* are not human beings, let alone Asians. Buddha, the Jade Emperor, and Guan Yin are divine beings. Monkey is an immortal ape; Piggy, a foolish, greedy pig-man; Sandy, a man-eating sand ogre; and White Dragon Horse is a sea dragon. Tripitaka (Xuanzang), the monk of the story, is the exception. If a school or university has the resources, the actor playing Tripitaka probably should be Asian.

Nevertheless, decisions about how to cast the characters of the play need to be addressed and decided both by students and faculty members. At a minimum, thorough discussions by students and faculty members of race, white privilege, and the various forms of subtle and overt forms of racism that are expressed toward Asians in the United States should be addressed in general and with specific regard to a work of art that is an essential part of Asian cultural heritage.

CONCLUDING OBSERVATIONS

This discussion of *The Journey of the West* has attempted to discuss the religious significance of the novel for Chinese culture and has provided examples of how it has supported the development of Chinese folk religion. Folk beliefs related to Monkey King are influential, and even some middle-class Hong Kong Chinese with university educations partly believe in some elements of Chinese folk religion, such as those associated with Shen Da.

For example, some will state that when an accomplished Shen Da boxer, such as one who had the ability to be possessed by a powerful god like Monkey King, becomes ill and dies, wounds will suddenly appear on his body in places where he was struck but not injured when alive. Of course, many contemporary Chinese are brought up within the context of a science-based education and are skeptical of the beliefs associated with Monkey King and religious beliefs in general. Other Chinese follow religious traditions besides those found in the novel.

It is important to emphasize in discussions of the novel at all grade levels, whether with elementary school students, middle school students, or undergraduates, that *The Journey to the West* is widely admired in Chinese culture and serves as the basis of religious belief and action for many Chinese people, but not all. Just as many people admire the poetic beauty and wisdom of the stories in the King James version of the Bible without believing in supernatural miracles, many Chinese enjoy the beauty, humor, wisdom, and excitement of *The Journey to the West* without being spiritual followers of the Monkey King.

REFERENCES

Amos, D. M. (2016, March 24). Lies I have told about martial artists: An introduction to fieldwork in martial arts studies [Blog post]. Retrieved from https://chinesemartialstudies.com/2016/03/24/doing-research-5-lies-i-have-told-about- martial-artists/.

Becker, H. S. (2015). *Becoming a marihuana user*. Chicago: University of Chicago Press.

Billinge, T. (2018). The Temple Trail–Hong Kong. [Blog post]. Retrieved from https://thetempletrail.com/category/countries/hong-kong/.

Dudbridge, G. (1970). *The Hsi-yu-Chi: A study of antecedents to the sixteenth-century Chinese novel*. Cambridge: Cambridge University Press.

Fu, J. S. (1977). *Mythic and comic aspects of the quest: Hsi-yu Chi as seen through Don Quixote and Huckleberry Finn*. Singapore: Singapore University Press.

Jordan, D. K. (2012). 神.鬼.祖先：一個台灣鄉村的民間信仰 (*Gods, ghosts and ancestors: Folk religion in a Taiwanese village*). Taiwan: 聯經出版公司.

Lattimore, D. (1983, March 6). Review of Anthony C. Yu's translation of the complete "Monkey": *The Journey to the West*. *New York Times*. Retrieved from http://www.nytimes.com/1983/03/06/books/the-complete-monkey.html?pagewanted=all.

Nason, B. (2003). *The journey plays*. Fortitude Valley, Australia: Playlab Press.

Overmyer, D. L. (1998). *Religions of China: The world as a living system*. San Francisco: HarperCollins.

Roberts, M. (2014). *Three kingdoms: A historical novel*. Berkeley: University of California Press.

Ross, H. (2005). *Literacy for life: China, a country study*. New York: UNESCO. Retrieved from http://unesdoc.unesco.org/images/0014/001461/146108e.pdf.

Waley, A. (1943). *Monkey, folk novel of China*. London: George Allen & Unwin.

Walker, H. (1998). A look at the origins of the Monkey Hero Sun Wukong: Indigenous or foreign? *Sino-Platonic Papers*, *81*(September), 1–110.

Ward, B. E. (1979). Not merely players: Drama, art and ritual in traditional China. *Man, New Series*, *14*(1), 18–39.

Young, E. (2001). *Monkey king*. New York: HarperCollins.

Yu, A. C. (1977, 1978, 1980, 1983). *The journey to the west* (Volumes I, II, III, IV). Chicago: University of Chicago Press.

Zhang, T. (2006). *Literacy education in China*. New York: UNESCO. Retrieved from http://unesdoc.unesco.org/images/0014/001462/146208e.pdf.

Chapter 5

Reading *Sadako* with Third Graders

Trina Lanegan

This chapter recounts a unit taught in a third-grade classroom in a rural US school district about the story *Sadako* by Eleanor Coerr (1977). Sadako's story is a powerful one, even sixty-two years after her death. It contains significant global content and can be mined by new and veteran teachers alike depending on the students' ages and grades.

POWER OF TEACHERS

Teachers have immense power of choice and, often, wide latitude when it comes to choosing the stories and books students hear and read. When educators have a mandate to teach about "Asia" or "Japan" in elementary school, this looks very different from classroom to classroom, school to school, and district to district. Within one small, rural elementary school with three separate same-grade classrooms, children will receive different experiences in learning simply by virtue of which teacher they have and that teacher's worldview and use or neglect of international and global literature.

What urgency or compulsion motivates educators to open the curriculum to students in a way that broadens their understanding of the world? Childhood is the time when concrete ideas and experiences become the foundation of who one later becomes. This also makes it the ideal time for exposure to the world beyond the family and community. For this reason, it is imperative that educators introduce international and global literature to children as early as possible. The use of international and global children's literature on a daily, regular basis is one place to begin.

The practice of reading aloud to students daily is a hit-or-miss reality in elementary classrooms. It can depend on the values and priorities of individual teachers, their daily schedule, and the mandated and suggested uses of curriculum. All of these variables will impact whether or not students hear a read-aloud and whether it is used instructionally as an integrated literacy component. What used to be a protected and almost sacred elementary school practice—listening to your teacher read aloud to the class daily—is, however, now an exception.

Many teachers have abandoned this in favor of designated computer learning in which students, for example, use math fluency programs to build their computational skills. Since this is a now popular daily activity, any time students spend on the computer is usually viewed as imperative to learning. These skill-building, content-specific activities have become a prized and sometimes mandated elementary classroom activity, viewed as an important practice geared toward student achievement. Elementary teachers must cover the entire curriculum and sometimes feel compelled to add other subjects like keyboarding instruction or even teaching chess.

The reality is that elementary school teachers have much content to teach and assess with real time constraints. Reading aloud children's literature, international or not, for even fifteen minutes a day can seem like a luxury. However, teachers know that when students hear a read-aloud they are able to enjoy and understand stories that otherwise they may not be able to read to themselves. The read-aloud creates access to exceptional books often too difficult for the child to read independently. Teachers also know that when children are read aloud to on a regular basis their motivation and interest for reading increases. Fisher and Frey (2016) state that "read alouds . . . promote engagement and foster critical thinking skills in content area instruction" (p. 43).

Of all the pressures on teachers at the primary and elementary levels, teaching students to read is one of the most crucial but challenging. This challenge alone should propel new and veteran teachers alike to become familiar with the best in international and global literature for children and motivate them to creatively integrate these stories into the mandated content units. Texts from a diverse array of global communities and cultures should match the themes and content. The use of global literature, the literal reading of another culture's stories, begins to open the wider world to the listening child.

In a third-grade science unit on plants, a global story on bee keeping is fascinating for students and shows that people in another place care about the environment and sustainability of their communities and the planet. A story from a culture other than their own can show children that people work hard every day to provide meals and housing for their family, and yet how this is accomplished can be radically new information for students in their content study of economics.

During a unit on energy, reading *The Boy Who Harnessed the Wind* (Kamkwamba & Mealer, 2016) as an integrated literacy component will open the world to the students in a way like no other text can, illustrating the application of ingenuity in the face of hardship with the use of science.

It is imperative that teachers take the time to plan what international literature they will infuse and integrate into their mandated and self-created units throughout the school year. Intentional planning is essential. In addition to integrating international literature as a component, children's literature itself can be the focus of the study, as was the case in the teaching of *Sadako* (Coerr, 1977).

Another reason that teachers resist or do not include international children's literature in the classroom is that they may not possess an urgency for the value of exposing children to information about people outside of their own country. Regardless of the fact that story titles are available at the school library or downtown at the public library, many do not utilize these resources. In my experience, some teachers consider this kind of teaching a waste of time.

Some teachers even resent the diversity in their own classrooms and voice objections to fellow staff members about why, for example, all their students cannot speak English. This is a constant source of anger and frustration for some teachers. If some American teachers resent the challenges they face in "doing school" with children who speak languages in addition to English, these same teachers do not feel compelled to introduce other languages, cultures, and histories in books and stories. Regardless of these challenges and resistance to the use of global and international children's literature, one would strongly argue that it must be used anyway.

If a goal of education is to create graduates who are global citizens who can compete and cooperate with people from other nations, students must become deeply acquainted with cultures other than their own. Because global cultures consist of fellow human beings, students who learn about other cultures can apply their knowledge to build bridges among people, communities, and nations. Learning about other cultures is one of the most powerful ways to reduce hate-based violence.

SADAKO'S STORY

Sadako (Eleanor Coerr, 1977), a children's book written by an American author and illustrated by Ed Young, is about a devastating period in world history. It is the poignant story of a sixth-grade girl who loves to run track, enjoys school, and cares deeply for her family. She becomes ill with "radiation sickness" due to her exposure at the age of two to the Hiroshima atomic bomb. Her story illustrates her courage and that of her family in the face of sadness and loss.

It is likely that few American elementary students in rural schools know much about the US president's decision to use atomic bombs against Japanese citizens in Hiroshima and Nagasaki at the end of World War II. This may be because teachers are not comfortable with the history of America's participation in the making and dropping of the atomic bomb. Teachers may not see a connection, or choose to make one, between Sadako's story and its historical context. The questions that the third graders described in this chapter ask are challenging for adults to explain. The US government's actions and decisions during World War II can be difficult to defend.

Why read this book to eight- and nine-year-old children in a school setting? One could teach about contemporary Japan and omit this section of history. However, third-grade students can understand historical facts within well-designed content units.

READING *SADAKO* WITH THIRD GRADERS

A class of third graders read *Sadako* (Coerr, 1977) in a teacher-designed read-aloud unit modeled and adapted from a curricular approach called Collect-Interpret-Identify (CIA)[1] (Collinge, 2011). A variety of books from various genres are used in the CIA model. Having just completed the realistic fiction title *The War with Grandpa* (Smith, 1984) with this same class, the students were ready to step into a historical fiction book with Sadako's story. Themes of right and wrong, war and peace, friendship and family found in *The War with Grandpa* (Smith, 1984) set a foundation and created a natural continuity for the historical novel *Sadako*.

The goal was to use the story to build literacy with a group read-aloud, integrating vocabulary study, guided oral language, and writing. Another goal was to explore and introduce the theme in the historical context of the Hiroshima bombing during World War II, building from the learning just completed from *The War with Grandpa* (Smith, 1984). Another intention was to use the story to expose students to broader story concepts embedded in the book like illness and disease, friendship in the face of hardship, and war and peace.

The story of Sadako is grade appropriate for third graders, and its content created a vehicle for literacy learning within social studies content. Learning was scaffolded using graphic organizers, oral sentence frames, and stems. Sentence frames scaffold students as they share their ideas, beliefs, opinions, and understanding of the text and learning. For those students who literally do not know how to begin, the sentence frame and stem choices are an open hand for language expression. These were posted in the classroom within view and accessible to all students.

The *Sadako* unit took place at the end of the school year, after the third graders had been using a variety of sentence frames, stems, and supports through the reading of three other CIA books. Some of the students had memorized and internalized the CIA sentence frames that said, for example, "When the book said _____, I thought _____" (Collinge, 2011, p. 142).

Collinge (2011) writes that she and her colleague designed the sentence frames and stems for what she calls Turn and Talk opportunities to promote oral language during daily text reading. Collinge also explained that she needed a routine she could use with her students that "would be authentic, one that mimicked the back and forth sharing of ideas found in real-life conversations" (p. 14). This idea of creating space for children to have "real-life conversations" shows intentionality that promotes oral language and also deep comprehension.

It is in these moments of peer-to-peer dialogue when new learning and comprehension can occur. When one student listens to his/her classmate describing his/her thinking around a character's inner hope for survival, as in *Sadako*, what can transpire is something as complex as learning about empathy. The fact that the story is set in another time period and in another country and culture is crucial.

A child could negotiate the meaning around another little girl who wanted to get better, so she folded paper into cranes to keep her hopes alive. What children taught others when they shared their ideas, thoughts, feelings, and understanding was vitally important. It can happen when teachers commit to creating spaces for dialogue and time to talk and write reflectively. Barone (2010) describes classroom environments in which children are guided to engage in conversations of "complex questions about text with no clear right or wrong answer" (p. 83). This kind of discourse was encouraged throughout the *Sadako* unit and integral to the daily learning.

Many vocabulary words and concepts unique to Sadako's story and her Japanese culture and history were introduced and developed during reading time. A visual wall showing photo copies of Hiroshima, photos of Sadako and her family, a map of Japan, and word cards and phrases depicting story vocabulary were used interactively (see Figure 5.1). Every day before the designated reading time, guided questioning about the prior learning took place. Children were handed new word cards and phrases each day, and the teacher gave explicit information to build background for the day's reading.

When the teacher used vocabulary words and phrases matching those written on a card held by a student, that child would come forward and place their card on the wall. Eventually, as Sadako's story progressed, so did the wall

Figure 5.1   Learning Wall.

of learning progress and grow, representing all the important story elements and vocabulary. Students understood that this wall represented their learning because it was an integral piece to the recap from the prior day's reading and introduction for each new day. Every day, upon reading *Sadako*, the third graders gathered on the carpet in front of the wall.

A quick review of the prior day's reading would take place, oral predictions about the upcoming chapter were expressed, and the reading would begin. When children wrote about their responses to the reading, they often did so on the carpet in front of the learning wall, using it as a visual reference, guide, and prompt. Right away in chapter 1, the vocabulary was rich and explanations were required for the readers. The family in the story attended the Peace Day celebration at the Atomic Dome, a building partially intact but never repaired after the Hiroshima bombing, as a testimony to the destruction of the event.

The learning wall was useful immediately as photo copies of Hiroshima before the bomb and after were shared, and a photo copy of the Atomic Dome was shown and photo copies of Buddhist priests, also mentioned in chapter 1, were displayed, discussed, and added to the wall. The importance of Peace Day was explained as a memorial celebration for the victims and their families of the atomic bombing that killed Sadako's grandmother. The Peace Day celebration is described in the book as including a carnival, food stalls, and fireworks.

Also in the story, paper lanterns are carried to the river, and the names of deceased family members killed by the atomic bomb were written within.

This was followed by a description of the beautiful tradition of lighting candles inside the lanterns and setting them afloat on the river. Chapter 1 introduces the theme of death juxtaposed with Sadako's health and youth. It sets the tone and scene for impending hardship with the author's use of images related to the bomb survivors and their fear of leukemia.

Chapter 5 finally explains the meaning of folding cranes—the important element needed to comprehend the story's significance. When Sadako's classmate, Chizuko, visits her in the hospital, she tells the story of the thousand paper cranes:

> "Don't you remember that old story about the crane?" Chizuko asked. "It's supposed to live for a thousand years. If a sick person folds one thousand paper cranes, the gods will grant her wish and make her healthy again." (Coerr, 1977, pp. 34, 36)

Sadako is described in the book as feeling "safe and lucky" with the golden crane near her. At the end of chapter 5, the text reads, "After visiting hours it was lonely in the hospital room. So lonely that Sadako folded more cranes to keep up her courage" (p. 39).

The students were encouraged to use the learning wall as a source of independent reading material. Students could use pointers and read aloud from the wall to themselves or one another to build their reading and to continue to review and comprehend the story content. The students could take blank pieces of paper and create their own map of Japan and copy photos, phrases, and word cards.

Many did incorporate these into their own reading and writing pieces. Some students used the wall of text as a guide or a steppingstone to their own writing. Student-made creations added to the living wall of text. There was palpable excitement that built, tempered with a sobriety as the story of Sadako was revealed through the chapter reading each day. Students were invested in the story and Sadako's outcome.

Would she race again with her school's track team as she had in chapters 1 and 2? Or would she never race again because of her illness? Would Sadako make one thousand paper cranes and have her wish to become healthy again granted, as described in the old Japanese tale? The students genuinely wanted to know and could be heard discussing story details and making predictions and statements to one another while lining up for lunch or heading out to recess each day.

Some days the students used their writing notebooks for creating story responses. The objective was to create a time for children to reflect in writing about the chapter reading of the day. Many themes are embedded in Sadako's story. The students could respond to ideas from the story involving the characters and could make connections to their own lives if so desired. The students had choices. The responses allowed for both fact-based writing and personal reactions to the text. Later each day after the dedicated read-aloud time, students could volunteer to share their writing with a classmate or the whole class.

In creating guided writing responses for children to use as reflection and comprehension-building tools throughout the unit; an intention was that some prompts be open ended and others be structured and explicit. For example, a writing prompt might be, "Write and explain why Sadako did not tell her parents that she was dizzy after track practice." Another more open-ended prompt would be, "Share your thoughts on Sadako's brother, Masahiro." In this intentional way, the students could choose to elaborate in some of their written reflections and in others less so.

As the more intense themes of the book became clear with the continued reading through the story, would there be children in the classroom for whom the content was too troubling? If students living with their own unique hardships became distressed by the story, they could feel a lack of support in an overwhelming moment. In the third-grade class, there was more than one child for whom personal hardship was a reality in their own life.

An opportunity to engage in written responses to the chapter reading could mitigate and manage this, so that students could write factual responses to the story such as "I learned that Japan has a religion that honors relatives" as well as a more subjective response such as "I liked Sadako's friend at the hospital. I'm sad that Kenji died." Writing thoughts and feelings in a workshop model was a grade-appropriate vehicle for expression and reflection. When students shared their written responses with classmates, this provided another opportunity for reflection and potentially supported a discussion of difficult story themes.

STUDENTS' RESPONSES TO *SADAKO*

Throughout the unit, the students were encouraged and guided to discuss their thoughts freely.

Crane Folding

To build oral language and check for comprehension, the teacher asked, "What do you think of this story about the thousand paper cranes?" One of the students keyed in on the word *luck*, and a discussion ensued about shamrocks being lucky. Students compared the two symbols, applying their understanding of luck to the story.

This was an example of the students using their cultural lenses to negotiate new and different meanings of the concepts and symbols of luck and hope. As the class progressed through the book and each day students had peer conversations, some commented on Sadako's paper crane folding and wondered about its value in healing her. Even after Sadako's friend Kenji dies of leukemia in the hospital, and she acknowledges to the nurse her belief that she will die next, Sadako continues to fold cranes.

In writing responses some students expressed belief that Sadako was weakening herself further by folding cranes. Other children were invested in the hope of the paper crane story, and in their final writing, knowing the outcome of the story, they still wondered, "If you are sick will making a thousand paper cranes work to make you feel better?" Another student wrote about Sadako's fortitude. He said, "I know that when Sadako made all those paper cranes she felt really determined to finish all before she died."

Clearly, the students were concerned about the progression of Sadako's illness and wished that she would not die. It was interesting that two students felt that the act of folding cranes would accelerate Sadako's death and therefore, Sadako should stop folding. In that moment, the students seemed to have misunderstood the Japanese cultural significance of folding cranes.

Not having a custom to fold paper cranes for healing in their own culture and not deeply comprehending the cultural meaning of the folded cranes in the Japanese culture, the students focused on the literal act of making cranes with origami papers, overlooking the more significant cultural meaning in the story. Three children expressed in their writing the wish to know Sadako and have her teach them how to make cranes.

The wishes seemed separated from the wider application of the crane story and its implications for healing and hope. There was a disconnect in some students who were excited about the idea of Sadako doing origami, apart from her act of continual folding as a remedy for leukemia. Finally, one male student summed up his understanding around the paper crane story that helped other students to understand the true meaning of folding cranes.

He said that folding cranes provided Sadako with hope: "When Sadako made the paper cranes I thought that made her weaker and weaker, but it gave her hope and courage." After his comment, most children agreed with him and showed understanding for why Sadako kept folding cranes although she kept becoming weaker and weaker day by day. However, one child was not persuaded by his peers at all.

He wrote that folding the cranes "didn't bring good luck" and stated, "It was just for no reason at all. Why did she think the paper cranes would help her?" His reaction highlights the inability to empathize with Sadako and to see the situation from her viewpoint and experience. Although most students were reflective in their oral conversations with one another and in their written responses to the story, some were unable to move beyond literal comprehension. They did not make the inferences and synthesis that this particular story requires.

Medical Terms

Leukemia and radiation sickness were vocabulary necessary to define and explain. Children learned basic definitions for *radiation illness* and *leukemia*, as related to the bombs dropped on Hiroshima and Nagasaki. The students required explanations related to how cells can manifest in disease and illness even years after exposure to life-threatening substances. Besides Sadako, the two characters in the story who are ill and die are Sadako's Oba-chan (grandmother), who died on August 6, 1945, in the bombing; and Kenji, whom Sadako meets at the hospital and is ill.

Kenji believes the illness was passed to him from his mother and says, "The poison was in my mother's body and I got it from her" (Coerr, 1977, p. 44). Sadako was two years old when the Hiroshima bomb dropped and leukemia surfaced in her body at age eleven, nine years after exposure. There was some confusion in a few students about who in the story died from direct exposure to the bomb (Oba-chan and Sadako) and who died from leukemia as a result of their mother's radiation exposure (Kenji).

This confusion was one of the ways that learning new content was manifested, and the students needed to have time to discuss, question, and organize the layers involved in meaning making around the atomic bombings. We can imagine their thoughts: an atomic bomb, made by my country, was dropped on human beings and burned their skin; some of them died immediately, some died later, and some died because their mothers were exposed to radiation. All were difficult facts to comprehend, and thus, some misinterpretations resulted.

Gift to a Dying Child

When Sadako's mother made her a beautiful kimono and gave it to her to wear at the very end of Sadako's life, one student questioned this act. One commented, "This didn't make sense, why would she do that since Sadako was about to die?" A short, guided discussion followed. Parental love and tradition were offered as rationale for the kimono being made and given to Sadako, regardless of her illness. Afterward, most students argued against the student and stated that it didn't matter to Sadako's mother that her daughter was going to die. She wanted her daughter to have a beautiful kimono as this was part of their Japanese cultural tradition.

When students seek to make meaning from international stories, they do not always easily or readily understand another culture's values and traditions. Not knowing that wearing a beautiful kimono is every Japanese girl's passage to adulthood, some students had difficulty understanding why Sadako's mother did so. Misreading Sadako's mother's intent certainly would have caused a misreading of the entire story.

Creating opportunities to talk to one another in response to the story helps. Peers can reveal to one another their understanding, and the teacher can guide and provide students with a time and place for wrestling with meaning. It does not mean that every child will see things similarly or even accurately, but it is an important piece to children beginning to see beyond themselves, their community, and culture.

Blame

As the story ended and the outcome for Sadako was revealed, layered personal, family, and even nationalistic reactions surfaced from the students. In discussions, the children offered opinions and thoughts ranging from everything to questions about what Sadako's afterlife might be like to exactly how many extra paper cranes had been made by her classmates to reach one thousand.

The students responded in writing as an end-of-story assignment. The culmination of their understanding was revealed in this written evidence. The prompt was open-ended. They were asked to give their reaction to the story or to explain what they had learned. Many wrote both. Some students wrote opinion papers, and others wrote a summary of what they had learned. Some children wrote letters to characters, primarily Sadako and Masahiro (Sadako's brother).

Almost every child assigned fault for Sadako's death to either Japan or the United States. At no point during the instructional planning or learning time were the words or direct concepts of blame or fault introduced or explicitly covered. In other words, this was not an intentional outcome or planned focus of learning. An effort was made to portray the story as neutrally as possible based on the historical facts with no attempt to side with one country over another.

For example, factual information about the bombing was retrieved from a children's history website, a resource embedded in the CIA curriculum and used with the other read-aloud books. In addition, a simple timeline of the events around the end of World War II was discussed, including the fact that Germany had surrendered to the Allies in May 1945 but Japan had not.

Although the fact that the students focused on blaming either country or both shows their use of inference and critical thinking, it also highlights how difficult it is to teach historical fiction to American elementary children. Some students know how to detect clear cause and effect but are not necessarily accustomed to reading about and readily comprehending something as ambiguous as a story involving a real girl who dies of the effects of an atomic bombing. As a result, it seems that the majority of students decided that one country or another had to be at fault for this girl's death.

This may indicate that the students were disturbed by the cause of Sadako's death to the extent that they felt the need to place blame for her death. The student responses to the facts of Sadako's story reflected their shock and sadness, some directed at their own country's involvement in her death. This could have resulted in feelings of defensiveness, nationalism, or regret. The student writing reflected these strong reactions.

The written responses were personal and provided an authentic inside look at what each student was thinking and what they had comprehended about the story. Three of the students stated that Japan was to blame for the bombings on Hiroshima and Nagasaki. In other words, it was their own fault. The sole student who placed direct and explicit blame said, "I feel like the U.S.A. did the right thing because the Japanese started it by bombing Pearl Harbor." A small sketch of an American flag followed this sentence.

Two others who blamed Japan for the bombings framed their expression of this as wishes; for example, "I wish that Japan had surrendered" so that Sadako did not die. There was no reference to Pearl Harbor in the book. The teacher referenced it briefly within the use of the World War II timeline. Therefore, these students' references to Pearl Harbor illustrated that they used their own cultural lenses to express values and perspectives from their own background knowledge in the final writing responses.

Three children expressed that it was both Japan's and the United States's fault that the bombing occurred and that Sadako subsequently died. One of the students stated that Japan had bombed Pearl Harbor so that is why it was their fault that the atom bomb was dropped on Hiroshima and Nagasaki. She continued that the United States should have warned Japan that not only would they be bombed but also that it would be an atomic bomb. She then immediately expressed outrage that the bomb had to be an atomic bomb: "I mean, why an atom bomb?"

A second student who blamed both the United States and Japan for Sadako's death also wrote that America should have warned the Japanese an atomic bomb was coming. The instruction during this unit did include mentioning of the leaflets dropped prior to the bombing. This fact was not highlighted above others but was included in a timeline of events at the end of World War II. Evidently, the Hiroshima bombing story had a deep impact on the student readers.

Fifteen students out of the class of twenty-four assigned blame and disbelief toward the United States for dropping the atomic bombs. One student stated that "innocents" had been killed and that this was unacceptable.

Another student said in his opening sentence, "I think it was America's fault" that Sadako died. Student responses indicated that the bombings were almost unimaginable. The sentences, "I can't believe that America would drop the atomic bomb," and "This is the saddest story" were examples of this disbelief.

War and Peace

One student expressed concern for Mrs. Sasaki and wondered how she could overcome the death of her daughter. Another child praised Masahiro as a good brother for hanging the paper cranes in Sadako's hospital room and for visiting her there. Another student described Sadako as "the most heroic girl." Six student responses showed conflicting thoughts. The students were negotiating blame, surprise, disbelief, sadness, and morality.

Some of the students made assertions like, "I believe war is wrong and peace is right," and "War is bad, peace is good." Connecting to prior learning gained from the previous read-aloud, many of the third graders used direct quotes and language from the book *The War with Grandpa* (Smith, 1984). The most frequently used were "War brings misery," and "Only a fool wants war."

All children made at least one assertion that war is bad and peace is desirable, regardless of the style of their writing and whether they assigned blame for the bombings on Sadako's death or not. One student wrote it was too bad that Japan did not get "payback" for the bombings. Another student said violence is never a good way to solve problems and that people should just forgive each other. Two students pointed out that other people besides Sadako had died in the Hiroshima and Nagasaki bombings, and three children did not include any language about either country at all. All of the students expressed in one way or another regret that Sadako had died.

This aspect of the student responses fell into ruminations and questions on death and the afterlife. Some of the children expressed their "wish" that Sadako had not died. One student wrote that Sadako was now "in the clouds," and in those papers addressed as letters to Sadako, examples of questions were: "Do you see Kenji?" and "Do you know we will never forget you?" One girl wrote, "Finally, the last problem was that Sadako died. This is my favorite part because you feel happy and know that she is real and that she will always be flying in the wind with all the paper cranes."

The students' assertions seemed to go beyond clichés. Many children expressed that if she had not died they might have learned the art of origami from Sadako and folded paper cranes with her. There seemed to be no distance, as if the students were writing to another child they had met and knew. Time, space, and even death did not prevent the third graders from writing in detail about what they would do if only Sadako had lived. They wished to be her friend, learn her language, visit her, and play with her.

REFLECTIONS AFTER TEACHING *SADAKO*

The student responses to the story of Sadako were honest and direct. The life and death of a real child was revealed to children who live in a different time and culture. Throughout the reading of the story, the children discussed their feelings, opinions, and reactions. The planning was intentional, with best literacy practices and research-based methodologies and strategies for learning in view, and there was a high level of focus and apparent motivation on the part of the students.

The prevalent responses could be organized under these categories: perspectives on war and peace, wishes, questions, and facts learned. The topic of death especially impacted the students. Internal conflict about the sadness and the cause of Sadako's death were difficult for some. Children cried on the day the chapter describing her death was read. Two days later when they completed their final papers this grief surfaced again in their writing.

Throughout the unit, the students were encouraged to voice and share their feelings and thoughts to each other. This pedagogical technique seems to have resulted in the students successfully reaching more culturally authentic readings by themselves. For example, when some students completely overlooked the significant meaning cranes and crane folding symbolized in Japanese culture, it was their peers who guided them to a more culturally nuanced reading.

When some students were puzzled that Sadako's mother gave her a beautiful kimono at the end of her life, it was the peers who again created a consensus about the cultural validity of this action, with a few prompts from the instructor. This highlights the power of free and unmonitored discussions among students themselves, not necessarily dictated by the instructor. It provides evidence that students are capable of negotiating unfamiliar cultural meanings and moving toward more culturally appropriate and sensitive reading of multicultural, global, and international children's stories.

The fact that third graders in a rural American school who did not know where Japan was located on a world map before the *Sadako* unit could engage in critical and synthesized discussions illustrates that even lower-elementary-level students can read and interpret stories that are culturally unfamiliar to them if the stories are of high quality and engaging. One caution, however, arose after the unit.

According to reader response theory, readers make meanings of the text out of both purely personal reactions and culturally conditioned ways of reading (see chapter 2 in the accompanying book *(Mis)Reading Different Cultures: Interpreting International Children's Literature from Asia* for more thorough discussions of readers' subjective interpretations). This point is most evident when the students came running out of the gate in their final written papers, assigning blame for Sadako's death with no prompting.

By doing so, the students inadvertently manifested their own individual forms of family values, perspectives on nationalism, and morality that resulted in not every student seeing the story in the same way. In fact, it did not seem to necessarily matter that the material was developed in as objective a manner as possible or that the instruction was intended as neutral. The students created their own interpretations by mustering all the historical knowledge they had beforehand and using their own cultural lenses to assess the story and make personal critiques and connections.

The purpose of Sadako's story is certainly not to blame either Japan or the United States. It is simply to portray the tragedy of war through the life of a Japanese girl. After reading the story, all the third graders expressed that war was wrong and peace was right. However, some students made their defensive and nationalistic comments about the bombing in Hiroshima explicit. Others were more concerned about the devastation people in Hiroshima suffered after the bomb rather than defending their own country's action.

This illustrates that the degree of empathy the students manifested through reading *Sadako* greatly differed. Empathy is a prerequisite for understanding cultural others from their points of view and is essential upon interpreting multicultural, global, and international literature in a culturally authentic way (see chapter 6 in the accompanying book *(Mis)reading Different Cultures: Interpreting International Children's Literature from Asia* for more thorough discussions of cultural empathy). In this sense, our attention should go to students' building empathy toward cultural others through various activities at school.

Reading multicultural, global, and international stories is one way to accomplish it. However, without educators demonstrating intentional and planned inquiries that purposefully build up empathy, constantly challenging their ways of thinking, students' levels of empathy could remain intact. If that is the case, reading stories about cultural others will have no purpose.

CONCLUSION

Challenging issues will arise when teachers use international and global children's literature in elementary classrooms to teach reading, writing, science, or social studies. Because children hold within themselves their own unique and powerful views of the world, typically through the lenses of their own culture and family values, learning about real events in history will be difficult for some, particularly when actors within their own culture are unveiled as engaging in historically troubling events.

These hurdles are, however, not a reason to abandon international children's literature. Children will learn from the stories and learn from one another about the wider world. The totality of learning may not be readily visible or measurable through assessment. However, the more we expose children to different cultural perspectives through multicultural, global, and international children's literature with an intention to build empathy toward cultural others, the more empathetic children will become. Teachers' intentional teaching on this matter, bears a social responsibility in the world that is increasingly interconnected.

NOTE

1. The unit using *Sadako* was teacher made and used the CIA approach as an adapted model. Because the unit was less than two weeks long, the primary CIA components used were collecting information about the story characters, setting, and time, and looking for the author's message and line of thinking, daily vocabulary instruction, summarizing, utilizing oral language sentence stems and frames, utilizing written sentence frames, finding the turning point, and writing about the reading.

The CIA approach was created by Sarah Collinge (2011) and is fully explained in her book *Raising the Standards through Chapter Books: The C.I.A. Approach*. It provides an entire structure for using children's literature for read-aloud instruction for the whole class.

REFERENCES

Barone, D. (2010). Comprehension in the primary grades. In K. Ganske & D. Fisher (Eds.), *Comprehension across the curriculum: Perspectives and practices K–12* (pp. 75–95). New York: Guilford Press.

Collinge, S. (2011). *Raising the standards through chapter books: The C.I.A. approach*. Seattle, WA: Peanut Butter Publishing.

Fisher, D., & Frey, N. (2016). *Improving adolescent literacy: Content area strategies at work* (4th ed.). Boston, MA: Pearson.

CHILDREN'S LITERATURE CITED

Coerr, E. (1977). *Sadako*. Illustrated by E. Young. New York: G. P. Putnam's Sons.

Kamkwamba, W., & Meager, B. (2016). *The boy who harnessed the wind*. Illustrated by A. Hymas. London: Penguin Random House.

Smith, R. K. (1984). *The war with grandpa*. New York: Yearling.

Part II

ANNOTATED BIBLIOGRAPHIES OF INTERNATIONAL CHILDREN'S LITERATURE FROM SELECTED ASIAN COUNTRIES

Chapter 6

Annotated Bibliographies of International Children's Literature from Selected Asian Countries

CHINA/TAIWAN, BY MIAO YING (JANET) CHEN

Mooncakes, by Loretta Seto. Victoria, Canada: Orca Book, 2013.

Summary of Three Stories of the Moon Festival

This story begins as the main character stays up late with her parents to celebrate the Chinese Moon Festival. They light paper lanterns and hang them up on a tree. While drinking hot tea and eating mooncakes, her parents tell her three stories of the Chinese Moon Festival.

Hou-Yi the Archer

A long time ago there were ten suns in the sky and the world was hot and dry. The emperor asked his master archer, Hou-Yi, to help. Hou-Yi was the most skilled archer the world has ever known. He shot down the nine extra suns, and the world became a safe place. Hou-Yi was respected and honored everywhere as a hero, but within his soul he was a cruel and selfish person. He plotted to live forever, become the emperor, and control China and its people.

Because the emperor felt indebted to Hou-Yi for shooting down the extra suns, he gave Hou-Yi an elixir that would let him live forever. Hou-Yi's wife, Chang-E, learned of her husband's evil plans and consumed the elixir herself to prevent him from becoming the emperor. Afterward, Chang-E was spirited away to the moon where she forever lives.

The Lazy Woodcutter

Another person who lives on the moon is Wu-Gang. While he lived on Earth, Wu-Gang was a lazy woodcutter. He, too, hoped to learn the secret for eternal life, and while walking in the mountains one day he encountered an immortal being. Wu-Gang humbly greeted the immortal and begged to be taught the secret of eternal life. The immortal promised to teach Wu-Gang how to become immortal, but only if he studied hard and did everything that was asked of him. Wu-Gang agreed, but as soon as the lessons began he got bored and felt like taking a nap. It wasn't long before Wu-Gang lay down, fell asleep, and ceased learning the secrets to eternal life.

When the emperor heard what had happened he lost his temper and banished Wu-Gang to the Moon Palace. Wu-Gang was sent to the moon and told that he had to chop down a massive tree before he could return to Earth. The emperor warned Wu-Gang that if he stopped chopping he would die. Although Wu-Gang had been chopping away at the giant Moon Palace tree all this time, it magically restores itself after every ax stroke. At this very moment Wu-Gang is still at work, chopping away as fast as he can.

Jade Rabbit

A long time ago three moon immortals wanted to test the goodness of the animals who lived on Earth, so they turned themselves into three poor men and went out begging for food. When they met Fox and Monkey, both had food to give them. When they met Rabbit he had no food, so Rabbit jumped into the fire to cook himself for their dinner. The three immortals were so touched by Rabbit's self-sacrifice they gave him new life at the Moon Palace, where he has become the eternal "Jade Rabbit."

Toward Authentic Interpretations

Readers might not understand the connection between the Chinese Moon Festival and the three stories of Chang-E, Wu-Gang, and Jade Rabbit. The Moon Festival falls on the fifteenth day of the eighth month of the lunar calendar, a calendar used for special occasions by the Chinese and people from several other Asian countries.

The lunar calendar is different from the solar calendar, which is also used by the Chinese and people in many other countries, including the United States. Using the lunar calendar ensures that the night of the Moon Festival always falls on a night with a full moon. Thus, people can have hot tea and mooncakes with their family while enjoying the view of a bright, full moon. Chinese people always say that they can see the shadows of Chang-E, Wu-Gang, and Jade Rabbit on the moon, and these three folktales are associated with the Chinese Moon Festival.

Readers also might not understand the reason why both Chang-E and Wu-Gang wanted to become immortal. In Chinese culture, similar to many other cultures, people want to look youthful and live forever, remaining eternally attractive and healthy. Therefore, many Chinese folktales contain elements of the desire for immortality. Moreover, in order to understand why the three immortals honored the rabbit's self-sacrifice by letting him live in the Moon Palace, the readers need to understand that the Moon Palace is a heavenly place referred to by the Chinese people as a fabulous wonderland of gods and immortals.

Celebrating the Dragon Boat Festival, by Sanmu Tang. Shanghai, China: Shanghai Press, 2010.

Summary

The main character, little Mei, knew that the day was a special day, but she didn't know why. She saw her dad hang some herbs at the front door and her grandma put some sachets around her neck. Little Mei's grandpa explained to her the meaning behind the Dragon Boat Festival.

Qu Yuan was a famous poet in ancient China during the Warring States period (475 BC–221 BC). He was respected and the king's loyal adviser. The king valued Qu Yuan's advice, but because of the favor the king showed him other courtiers became jealous. They said bad things about Qu Yuan, and the king came to believe the false rumors about him. Eventually, the king stopped listening to Qu Yuan and ordered him to leave the palace and return to his hometown.

With Qu Yuan gone, the king began listening to the bad advice of other advisers. Soon the king began to make serious mistakes that weakened the country and allowed it to be preyed upon by enemy nations. To protest the bad advice the king was receiving, Qu Yuan decided to end his life. He jumped into the Miluo River where he drowned on the fifth day of the fifth month of the lunar calendar.

Ordinary people admired the self-sacrifice and patriotism of Qu Yuan. When they learned where he had died they paddled their boats to that place on the Miluo River, beat drums, and threw rice into the water to distract the fish and prevent them from consuming his body. To this day the fifth day of the fifth month of the lunar calendar is when the Chinese people celebrate Qu Yuan's patriotism and sacrifice by paddling dragon boats and making rice dumplings in his honor.

Toward Authentic Interpretations

The topic of this book can be controversial to some teachers and students because suicide is considered a sin by some religions. To understand the story of Qu Yuan, readers must understand its cultural context. For many Chinese, similar to people in other nations, reputation and honor are more important than life itself. To protest the bad advice the king was receiving, Qu Yuan decided he must commit suicide. Most important to Qu Yuan was that the king rule wisely, and he felt that his own life was secondary. Qu Yuan's honor required that he sacrifice his life in order to gain the king's attention and change the erroneous path the monarch was taking the country.

Students can use the story of Qu Yuan to discuss why soldiers, police officers, and ordinary people sometimes bravely put their own lives at risk in order to save and protect other people and things larger than themselves.

While reading the book, students might not understand why the characters in the book hang the herbs and carry sachets around their bodies because the storybook did not explicitly explain it. The Dragon Boat Festival comes in May, which is the time when the weather starts to get hotter and insect-borne diseases begin to spread. It is believed that the smell of herbs and herbal sachets can prevent bugs such as mosquitoes from approaching. Chinese people also believe that some herbs look similar to swords, which can scare away evil spirits and prevent them from causing harm.

Auntie Tigress and Other Favorite Chinese Folktales, by Gia-Zhen Wang. New York: Purple Bear Books, 2006.

Summary

Once upon a time, there was an old tigress that had lived on Earth for so long she had mastered the skill of transforming herself into a human form. One day the tigress was hungry and wanted to find human beings to eat. She had heard that there was a girl, Mei Mei, whose mother was away from home working in another town, and whose auntie was coming over to take care of her and her sister. The tigress decided to eat the auntie first, and then pretend to be the auntie in order to sneak into the house and eat Mei Mei and her sister. Mei Mei had never seen her auntie before, so she opened the door for the tigress, who had transformed herself into an old lady and was wearing her aunt's clothes.

Although Mei Mei thought there was something strange about the tigress auntie's behavior, she did not worry too much about it. Suddenly, a mouse ran on to the table and tried to eat some buns. Tigress Auntie was furious about the appearance of the mouse, and her tail suddenly appeared from underneath her skirt and began to twitch. Mei Mei knew the auntie was really a tiger and decided to escape by telling Tigress Auntie that she wanted to use the toilet outside. Mei Mei met the mouse on her way out of the house. The mouse handed her three bags of sachets and told her to climb up a tree to prevent the tiger from eating her.

Realizing Mei Mei was trying to escape, Tigress Auntie chased her. Mei Mei was scared and threw all three bags of sachets at Tigress Auntie. The sachets suddenly transformed into thousands of red beans, mice, and needles, all of which hit Tigress Auntie head on and caused her to die.

Toward Authentic Interpretations

To have a better understanding of the story, readers must understand the Chinese cultural and social background and the meaning of each character. In Chinese society many people are poor and must leave their homes to find work and work outside their hometowns. While working in other towns, many Chinese parents leave their children to be cared for by relatives, such as grandparents, aunts, and uncles.

Tigers symbolize evil character in China, and Chinese parents tell their children to be careful of tiger monsters. Bags of herbs are used to drive away mosquitoes and other pests. Chinese also believe that these same herbal sachets can protect people from evil spirits and keep them safe. The story of Auntie Tigress has become one of the most famous Chinese folktales. It is especially used to educate young children about not opening the doors of their homes to strangers.

INDONESIA, BY TATI LATHIPATUD DURRIYAH

The Gift of the Crocodile: A Cinderella Story, by Judy Sierra. Illustrated by R. Ruffins. New York: Simon & Schuster Books for Young Readers, 2000.

Summary

This book is an Indonesian Cinderella story. It recounts a story of Damura, whose life of torment begins when her stepmother and stepsister move in her house and force her to do the chores of a servant. Later, Damura meets a magic helper, a grandmother crocodile who offers her help whenever it's needed. The grandmother crocodile is the guardian of the river. She comes to the surface upon hearing Damura crying for her lost sarong. The grandmother crocodile offers Damura help on the condition that she babysit a baby crocodile, in a test of her character. The baby crocodile is smelly and incessantly screams. Damura cradles the baby crocodile, ignoring its smell and noise. She passes the test and is rewarded with a beautiful sarong.

A jealous stepsister tries to replicate Damura's fortune by going to the river and pretending that she had lost a sarong, too. The grandmother crocodile offers her some help provided that the stepsister look after the same smelly and screaming baby crocodile. While looking after the baby crocodile, the stepsister grows impatience and spanks it. The grandmother crocodile is furious to see how badly the stepsister treats the baby crocodile. She gives the stepsister a beautiful sarong that soon turns into a rugged fabric that has leeches on it.

One day a prince holds a party in order to find a prospective wife. Damura turns to the grandmother crocodile for help. The grandmother crocodile outfits her with a sparkling gold sarong and blouse. Completing her elegant look is a pair of golden slippers. The prince immediately falls in love with Damura, but she has to depart hastily, leaving him a golden slipper as a clue. The prince finally finds her, and they marry.

Unable to overcome their jealousy, the stepmother and stepsister concoct a plan that nearly kills Damura. The grandmother crocodile saves Damura and sends the stepmother and stepsister off to a dark forest, and they are never seen again.

Classroom Applications

Crocodiles are large and fierce carnivorous reptiles that live in both freshwater and saltwater habitats. In the story they are referred to as guardians of the river. They typically have patience in waiting for their prey. For that reason, one ethnic group in Indonesia (Betawinese) characterized the crocodile as a symbol of loyalty and prosperity. In a wedding ceremony, the groom would bring a crocodile-shaped bread as a gift to his bride, symbolizing hope for a contented and long-lasting marriage.

Teachers could discuss the different kinds of magic helpers (like the grandmother crocodile) in variety of Cinderella stories told around the world and identify some of the traits that those magic helpers might symbolize. For example, the grandmother crocodile in this story symbolizes loyalty. In *Yeh-Shen*, a Chinese version of the Cinderella story, a koi fish represents the guardian of Yeh-Shen and symbolizes longevity and prosperity. What does the fairy godmother in Grimm's Cinderella story symbolize?

The Bird Hunter: An Indonesian Folktale, by Hearn Chek Chia. Illustrated by S. H. Kwan. Singapore: Alpha Press Ltd., 1972.

Summary

The Bird Hunter tells the story of a king who is passionate about archery and desires to marry off his daughter to the best archer. Upon hearing about the king's plan, a simple village man named Wajan sees an opportunity for him to marry the king's daughter. The only problem is Wajan knows nothing about archery, but he devises a strategy to impress the king. He travels to see the king and gives him one-eyed birds as a present. He says, "Your Majesty, I shot all my birds with my bow and arrow. I always shoot them in the eye." The king is impressed with Wajan and offers him his daughter in marriage.

During the wedding party, the king asks Wajan to demonstrate his archery skill in front of the guests. Upon hearing the request, Wajan nearly faints. He points the bow clumsily skyward. A man in the wedding party feels impatient with Wajan's clumsiness and suddenly slaps him on the back. Losing his grip on the bow, Wajan's arrow hits a bird on the neck, and it falls to the ground. Upon seeing this, the king is even more impressed with Wajan and tells him: "You are indeed the greatest archer I have ever seen."

After recovering from shock, Wajan says, "If that man hadn't hit me on the back I would have shot that bird in the eye and not on the neck." He declares, "I'm so disgusted I'll never touch a bow and arrow again." Indeed, Wajan never had to show his archery skill again, and he enjoys his marriage to the king's daughter.

Classroom Applications

Archery skills become the center of this story. In Indonesia, archery is strongly associated with a skill typically possessed by a ksatria, a noble and brave man with a warrior ethos similar to knights in Western countries. In Hindu epics from India that are influential in Indonesia, such as *Mahābhārata* (discussed in chapter 1 in this volume) and *Ramayana* (discussed in chapter 4 in this volume), there are many tales about noble ksatrias who learn or master archery skills. Arjuna, a main ksatria in the *Mahābhārata*, is said to have possessed the greatest archery skill of all. Indonesians love to invoke the symbol of Arjuna, a true ksatria and noble man.

Activities related to the story may include having students investigate other folk stories that make reference to archery skills. William Tell and Robin Hood are famous examples from the West. The Greek god Apollo is the god of archery in ancient Greek mythology, and Hou-Yi, as mentioned above, is the greatest archer of Chinese mythology. Students may also want to trace archers in modern tales, such as Katniss, a main character in the popular book and movie series *The Hunger Games*. J. R. R. Tolkien's *Lord of the Rings* has so many great archers it is difficult to determine which is the best.

The Mischievous Mouse Deer, Kanchil, by Kuniko Sugiura. In *Indonesian Fables of Feats and Fortunes*. Illustrated by K. Honda. Berkeley, CA: Heian, 2001.

Summary

The story's prologue aptly introduces readers to the main character Kanchil (most Indonesians spell it *Kancil*) as follows: "In Indonesia, there is an animal about half the size of a small deer. It is called a kanchil, which means mouse deer. The Kanchil in this story is very clever and likes to play tricks."

The story goes as follows: One day Kanchil was lost in a forest and encountered two of the fiercest animals there, an alligator and a tiger. Its first encounter with an alligator happened when Kanchil was figuring out how to cross a big river, and then how he could trick the alligator into helping him. Kanchil told the alligator he was not convinced that the alligator had many friends unless he saw them all at once.

Kanchil asked the alligator to call up his friends and to line up from one side of the river to the other so that Kanchil could count their number. The alligator and friends then made a line that was long enough for Kanchil to cross the river. Afterward, Kanchil tricked the same alligator twice more.

Encouraged by his success in fooling the alligator, Kanchil set out to challenge the fiercest beast in the forest, the tiger. One day Kanchil sat under a tree whose fruits were shaped like eggs but tasted extremely sour. A tiger passed by and wondered what Kanchil was doing. Kanchil said he was guarding "extraordinarily delicious [royal] eggs that only the king himself is allowed to eat." Being curious, the tiger wanted Kanchil to give him one, and he threatened to eat him if he didn't. Kanchil pretended to obey the tiger, but before the tiger ate the sour fruit he begged the tiger to let him go.

Once Kanchil galloped away, the tiger took a big bite of the fruit. "Aiiiieeee, it's sour!" the tiger screamed. His mouth was numb, and he couldn't enjoy eating for quite some time. The second time they met, the tiger was furious and ready to eat Kanchil. Again, with his cleverness, Kanchil was able to fool the tiger, and Kanchil once again escaped from that fierce beast.

Classroom Applications

Kanchil is known for his small yet cunning figure. He possesses speed and a clever thinking. Kanchil employs his intelligence to triumph over animals more powerful. Kanchil's character, of small size but with brains enabling it to outsmart much bigger creatures, is meant to amuse young children. The story's moral concerns the virtue of having a clever mind, something that is more important than physical size and strength.

It is important to note that in other Kanchil stories, pride in his speed sometimes weakens his judgment, especially when dealing with even smaller animals. In a story that is parallel to Aesop's *The Tortoise and the Hare*, Kanchil challenges a tortoise to race. Underestimating the significance of the tortoise's steady pace, Kanchil takes frequent rests along the racetrack. Before he realizes it, the tortoise reaches the finish line ahead of him.

The moral of Kanchil's character is that his clever thinking and speed are virtues, especially when it comes to dealing with larger and more powerful animals. In many cases Kanchil would win. But those virtues could become his weaknesses, especially when he competes with smaller and seemingly weaker animals. His speed could blind him into underestimating others, and he would eventually lose.

In discussing fables like the Kanchil story, teachers may invite students to identify personality traits associated with animals that they know or have heard about. For example, in Indonesia, Kanchil is associated with speed and fast thinking, and similar to Western folktales, foxes are typically thought of as being cunning and deceptive, and donkeys are described as slow thinking and lazy.

Cap Go Meh, by Sofie Dewayani. Illustrated by E. Gina. Indonesia: Litara Foundation, 2014.

Summary

Nisa and Lily are close friends from two different ethnic backgrounds. Nisa is Muslim from the Melayu background—the largest ethnic group in Indonesia who claims to be the indigenous people of the archipelago. Lily's ancestors were of Chinese origin, one of the minority ethnic groups in Indonesia.

One day Nisa shared to Lily about her experience with her favorite food called Cap Go Meh served during a Muslim's festive day Eid (a religious holiday for Muslims that marks the end of Ramadan). Nisa cheerfully recalled how she enjoyed eating Cap Go Meh along with her family. After attentively listening to what Nisa had to say about Cap Go Meh in her family tradition, Lily interjected by telling about the cultural tradition of Cap Go Meh in the Chinese community's culture. Lily explained to Nisa that Cap Go Meh is a cuisine specifically prepared during Chinese New Year. In fact, the food is one of the few essential elements during a two-weeks-long New Year celebration.

Soon after both tell each other about their experiences with Cap Go Meh, they engage in a disagreement about who would be the legitimate owner of the Cap Go Meh tradition. Both Nisa and Lily insist in claiming the right owner of the Cap Go Meh tradition. Toward the end of the story, however, they end up concurring with each other, declaring that aside from the question of where the origin of the food came from, Cap Go Meh is a favorite food for both of them.

Classroom Applications

Cap Go Meh is a cuisine served in many Indonesian family's homes and is available in many Indonesian restaurants. Its popularity signals the influence of the Chinese, which has been part of the country long before the Indonesian War of Independence (1945–1949) and Dutch recognition of Indonesian independence in 1949. In fact, when the Dutch arrived in Java early in the seventeenth century, major Chinese settlements had already existed along the north coast of that island for two centuries. As Rafferty (1984) notes, contacts were frequent between Java and the Chinese province of Fujian from the thirteenth century onward, allowing Gresik and Surabaya to develop important Chinese settlements by 1411.

As a multiethnic nation, Indonesia's influences came from diverse cultures (India, China, and Europe) and a variety of religions and belief systems including Islam, Animism, Hinduism, Confucianism, Buddhism, and Christianity. Food is arguably one distinctive indicator that shows the blending nature of Indonesian culture: it is made up of many cultural influences. The moral of the story rests on seeking a common ground among ethnic groups within Indonesia so that they could live harmoniously in mutual coexistence.

Cap Go Meh originated within the local Chinese cuisine of Indonesia and has become a popular food for Indonesians of many ethnic backgrounds. In using this story, teachers in the United States may engage students by discussing some of the influences of Asian cultures in food served in the United States. They may begin to identify a range of Asian influences in their school cafeteria, such as condiments like soy sauce (almost considered a staple in Asia like ketchup in the United States), or recipes such as chicken teriyaki noodle, which are available in many California public school menus, not to mention a basic staple such as rice, which was originally cultivated in Asia.

In addition to Asia, teachers may also want to talk about the influences of food from other parts of the world in the US diet, such as food that originated from Central and South America, the Middle East, Africa, and Europe.

Reference

Rafferty, E. (1984). Language of the Chinese in Java: An historical review. *The Journal of Asian Studies*, *43*(2), 247–72.

JAPAN, BY YAE TAKIMOTO HITE AND KATRINA MANAMI KNIGHT

Kaguyahime: The Tale of Bamboo Cutter, by D. Lear. Los Angeles: Firestone Books, 2013.

Summary

One day, a poor bamboo cutter came across a shining stalk of bamboo in the course of his work. He cut it open, and inside he found a baby girl no larger than his thumb. He and his wife named the girl Kaguya and raised her as their daughter as they were childless. As she grew she became more and more beautiful, and many suitors including the emperor attempted to win her love. Meanwhile, every night when the moon rose, Kaguya stared at it with longing.

Eventually, she revealed that her true home was the moon, and the day was soon approaching when she would have to return. When the day came, the moon people arrived and took Kaguya away, leaving all others in sadness.

Toward Authentic Interpretations

Taketori Monogatari originated from the tenth-century Japanese story. In Western societies, stories related to the moon tend to be associated with science fiction. Throughout Asia however, there is a custom of appreciating and worshipping the moon, some of which is represented by midautumn festivals and the existence of the lunar calendar. Because of this, the fact that Kaguyahime came from the moon illustrates that she was divine. Upon interpreting, readers of this story would need to consider this aspect of the culture that this story is written in and not to get caught up with technical parts of the story, such as how Kaguyahime was placed in the bamboo.

Some of the suitors used in the story were taken from actual historical figures who had great power and wealth in the Nara era. This story uses a couple of poor bamboo cutters as the fortunate people who receive Kaguyahime as earthly parents. This story uses people with power and wealth as suitors who cannot partake in what the couple have received, illustrating an irony of society in the Nara era which, like all state-level societies throughout history, there were significant power gaps among classes.

Kaguyahime also highlights some teachings of Buddhism. Most notably it illustrates the virtue of renunciation and acceptance of one's faith no matter how difficult such an act would be. Kaguya's parents finally accepted that she needed to return to the moon although this was something they refused to accept at the beginning. Their acceptance is also a symbol of their unconditional love for their daughter.

Urashima Taro: The Fisherman under the Sea, by M. Matsutani. Illustrated by C. Iwasaki. Bel Air, CA: Parents' Magazine Press, 1969.

Summary

One day, returning from his work, Urashima Taro, a young fisherman, saves a small turtle that was being tortured by a group of children, and he returns the turtle to the sea. The following day, he meets a giant turtle who tells him that the small turtle was in reality the daughter of the Emperor of the Sea and wants to thank him for this good deed. The turtle takes Urashima Taro to the bottom of the sea where he meets the Emperor of the Sea and his daughter.

Urashima Taro stays in the sea kingdom for three days, enjoying great luxury. He then asks to go home where his aging parents live. The Emperor of the Sea and the princess agree, giving him a precious box that he must never open. Urashima Taro agrees to this and is returned to the shore by the giant turtle. However, upon entering his village, he finds that everything has changed and he knows no one. Questioning the villagers, he is told that it has been three hundred years rather than three days; everyone he knows has been dead for centuries. Puzzled and grief stricken, Urashima Taro absentmindedly opens the box and immediately ages; inside the box were all the years of his life.

Toward Authentic Interpretations

Taro's kind actions to a small turtle in this story ironically result in an unhappy life, brought about by a display of human weakness. At the bottom of the ocean, Urashima Taro is treated as a special guest and enjoys himself, having forgotten his daily obligations at home for a while. This short-term pleasurable time in the ocean with the princess is hundreds of years on Earth. Also, Urashima Taro opens the box he received from the princess that he was told not to open. This caused him to age all at once, as if he had spent all those years on Earth. This display of human weakness in resisting curiosity draws comparison to Pandora's box.

This story is similar to a Western story, *Rip Van Winkle*, which depicts a different outcome for the main character than *Urashima Taro*. A Dutch villager named Rip Van Winkle lives in a rural area of New York State.

One day he wanders into the woods, runs into a group of short, bearded men with whom he plays nine-pins, and receives a drink that causes him to fall asleep. When he wakes up and goes down to his village, he finds out that twenty years have passed; his wife has passed away and the Revolutionary War has been completed, with the result that a new nation and national government have been established.

In this American story, the motivation of Rip Van Winkle for going into the woods was to take a break from his nagging wife. Contrary to *Urashima Taro*, Winkle's escape from reality and daily obligations leads him to rather a peaceful ending. He was released from the daily pressures directed toward him by his wife and also missed the violence and suffering associated with the Revolutionary War.

Kasajizo: Hats for the Jizos, by M. Matsutani, F. Matsuyama, and D. Tamaki. Singapore: Twinkle Tales for Kids, 2002.

Summary

The Japanese folk tale *Kasajizo*, like many others, features a poor old couple who live in the mountains. The husband was a hatter, but one winter the snow was so deep that he could not go out and gather sedge to weave his hats with. As he and his wife prepare dinner with what little rice they have, a baby mouse comes out from a hole in the wall crying from hunger. Feeling sympathy, the couple shares their meal with it and the other mice.

The following morning, they find that the mice had gathered a huge pile of sedge for them, with which they were able to make five hats. The old hatter took them into town to sell, and on the way there he notices that the six stone statues of Jizo-sama were covered in snow. He wipes the snow from their heads with the towel he wears on his own head, then continues on into the town.

However, he is not able to sell any hats and leaves feeling dejected. As he does, he sees that the statues are covered with snow again, and he wipes them clean, then carefully places a hat on each statue's head, but since there were only five hats and six statues, he gives the last statue his towel and continues home.

In the middle of the night, he and his wife are awaken by someone calling the old man's name. They go outside and found that the speakers are none other than the Jizo-sama statues who have pulled a sled loaded with food. They thank the hatter for his kindness, then return to their place by the road. The hatter, his wife, and the mice feast, then make offerings to the Jizo-sama statues for their kindness.

Toward Authentic Interpretations

A Jizo is a statue made of stone placed by the side of the road in town and worshipped in Japanese Buddhism. Japanese people usually make a wish to

Jizo statues for protection and blessings for the neighborhood. Readers of this book need to know that in the Japanese culture, spirits of gods are believed to reside in physical objects, as is the case for Jizo statues. This is why *sama*, a word that is added after an individual's name to express respect and politeness to the person, is used to call the statues Jizo-sama. The concept of spirits residing in physical objects is reflected by the way the old man treats the six Jizo-sama.

The moral of this story is that the more you do good things, the more rewards you will receive, and that sincere and kind actions always come back with rewards. This reflects a Buddhist belief of karma, that both good and bad deeds are accumulated over one's life. This belief is illustrated through the hatter and his wife who, although they were living an impoverished existence, could still be generous toward others. This story also reflects Confucian beliefs—we should not be captured by greed but act on what is right. We should think about others first and do what is beneficial for them before thinking about ourselves, and our acts should be sincere and truthful.

Tsuru no ongaeshi: The Crane Maiden, by M. Miyoko. Illustrated by C. Iwasaki. Bel Air, CA: Parents' Magazine Press, 1968.

Summary

Like many other Japanese folk tales, *Tsuru no ongaeshi* features a childless old couple who live alone in the woods. The husband was going into town one day when he found a crane caught in a trap. Feeling sympathy for a fellow creature, he releases it and carries on. Late that night there is a knock on their door, and when the old man and his wife answer it they find a beautiful young woman on their step. She says that she had been traveling and was caught in a snowstorm, and she asks to spend the night. The couple acquiesces, and she stays with them for several days, as the snowstorm did not stop. Eventually, she asks them to adopt her and the couple agrees, delighted by her good manners and kindness.

In thanks for their hospitality, she asks to weave a cloth for them to sell, but she must be alone in the room when she does so. The couple agrees, and a few days later she emerges with a beautiful cloth, which they are able to sell for a great deal of money. Not long afterward, she weaves a second cloth, again telling them to leave her in the room and not look inside. This cloth is even more stunning and sells for a higher price. The couple asks her for a third cloth, and she agrees.

Curious, they peek in the door this time as she is weaving and are stunned to see a crane pulling out its own feathers to weave into the cloth. It is clear from the state of its wings that it had already plucked out a great number of its feathers for the previous two cloths. Realizing their intrusion, the crane confesses that she is both their adopted daughter and the crane the old man had saved. Now that her identity has been discovered, she can no longer stay and be their daughter, so she flies away.

Toward Authentic Interpretations

In Japan cranes are a symbol of long life. For example, there is a custom of bringing one thousand origami cranes in prayer to somebody ill to help them recover (as discussed in chapter 5). By tradition, in Japan cranes are associated with longevity in people and have come to represent Japan itself.

At first, this story might seem to be teaching that good deeds are rewarded, as is believed in Japanese Buddhism. However, what the story mainly communicates is that humans can be too curious and should resist investigating things that they should not know.

The part in which the disguised crane sacrifices her own body to thank the old couple illustrates the virtue of putting others first before yourself, as is valued in Confucianism. In valuing self-sacrifice for others, this story illustrates complicated human psychology through the old couple when they found out that their greed, wanting more beautiful clothes from their adopted daughter, actually cost her a great deal. On the other hand, it also teaches that there have to be reasonable boundaries for acts of kindness, as the crane was physically suffering for the sake of performing an additional act of kindness.

Anpanman Series, by Takashi Yanase. Tokyo: Froebel-Kan, 1973–2013.

Summary

Anpanman is a character in an animated cartoon TV and book series created by Takashi Yanase in 1973. *Anpanman* is popular among young children in Japan, and the series continues to be broadcast until this day. The word *Anpan* refers to a type of sweet bread pastry in Japan that is small and round with sweetened red bean paste inside. Anpanman's face is *Anpan*, as his name suggests. He was created and raised by a master baker and lives in his bakery.

Anpanman's mission is to help people in need around town and protect the community. He is equally kind to everyone, and he carries out what is right. He typically helps the elderly and protects children and the weak from the town troublemaker, Baikinman, an anthropomorphic germ who always tries to find ways to defeat Anpanman and cause communal chaos.

Anpanman is similar to Superman of DC Comics in that he has the power to strike, lift heavy objects, and to fly. Like the "Man of Steel," he also has some weaknesses. For instance, whenever he sees someone hungry he feels a compulsion to give them a part of his head, which is made of bread, to eat. However, this act of bodily sacrifice and kindness causes him to lose most of his strength. He also loses his strength when his head gets wet. When his head is damaged, usually his friends need to rescue him, while the master baker quickly bakes a new head to replace the wet or damaged one. This freshly baked head replaces the old one and immediately restores Anpanman's strength.

Toward Authentic Interpretations

The television cartoon series does not focus on Anpanman's feelings, nor does it try to present him as an invincible superhero. It mainly illustrates Anpanman's kindness and pursuit of justice and peace regardless of the cost on his end.

Anpanman helping others by feeding his head to those who are hungry may seem strange to many Westerners. After all, Western cartoon heroes do not let themselves be eaten in the normal course of their heroic activities. An analyst influenced by Catholic symbolism may think this is not so strange and believe that the master baker symbolizes God; that Anpanman represents a divine hero in the mold of Jesus, whose body is consumed by his followers in communion; and that Baikinman is an agent of the devil.

This would be a false analysis, however. Neither the master baker nor Anpanman are thought of as divine by Japanese viewers, while Baikinman, in addition to his nastiness, is humorous and also possesses a few positive characteristics. Anpanman's most important message for young children in Japanese culture is that they must always put others first in spite of the personal danger and cost to themselves.

Further, no matter how many times Baikinman does rotten things to Anpanman, Anpanman always forgives him and never attempts to destroy him. That is to say, villainy in the Anpanman series is not treated the same as in most children's cartoons in the West, which tend to have a Manichean perspective, where the hero is good, the villain is bad, and the universe is strictly divided into dualistic domains of good and evil.

PHILIPPINES, BY JORDAN PIANO

Abadeha: The Philippine Cinderella, by Myrna J. de la Paz. Illustrated by Y. Tang. Auburn, CA: Shen's Books, 2001.

Summary

When Abadeha is only thirteen her mother, Abadesa, becomes ill and dies. This leaves her father, Abak, and Abadeha behind. One day Abak sets out on a trip to another island, where he meets a widow who has two daughters. He later marries the widow. The stepmother immediately sees that her own daughters are plain and mean-spirited compared to Abadeha, and swears to herself that she will make Abadeha's life miserable.

The stepmother treats Abadeha harshly, making her work morning to night, cleaning the house, fetching water from the river, cooking all the meals, and tending the stove. Even when Adadeha is tired her stepmother hits her with a broomstick.

One day the stepmother orders her to wash two handkerchiefs until the white one becomes black and the black one is white, causing Abadeha to weep at the riverbank. Hearing Abadeha crying, the female spirit of the river appears and completes the impossible task for her.

The spirit also presents Abadeha with a beautiful sarimanok bird, which is unfortunately taken, cooked, and eaten her stepmother. When Abadeha buries the bird's feet at her mother's grave, the female spirits of the forests grow a beautiful, jewel-encrusted tree at the site. A prince arrives at the same site and puts golden rings from the jewel tree on his fingers. However, the prince's fingers swell so badly he cannot remove the rings, and only Abadeha can help him. She needs to go to the prince to help him but is blocked by her stepmother. Eventually, Abadeha overcomes her stepmother's control and saves the prince.

Toward Authentic Interpretations

Franz Boas, one of the founders of anthropology in the United States, noted that it would seem that mythological worlds have been built up only to be shattered again, and that new worlds were built from the fragments (Boas, 1898). The story *Abadeha: The Philippine Cinderella* has conflict and outcomes similar to Indo-European versions of the Cinderella story. However, the author of the Abadeha story has retold it within the context of traditional Philippine folklore, and readers need to have knowledge of Filipino cultural beliefs in order to truly understand the story.

For example, Abadeha reflects how a child in the Philippines should act in modern society. In most areas of the Philippines, children are raised to be humble, subservient, and hardworking in support of their families. It is also rare for parents to punish their child for making mistakes: they are more likely to give a threat but never carry it out. Abadeha's stepmother is much harsher. She hits her with a broomstick and promises even harsher punishment: "I will whip you with the tail of a stingray!"

In addition, animism, the attribution of a soul, thought, and feelings to plants, inanimate objects, and natural phenomena, is strongly evident in this story, such as when Abadeha is helped by the spirits of the river and the forest. European American readers with Christian backgrounds may not recognize how important it has been for Filipinos to hold on to traditional indigenous beliefs during the series of colonial conquests they faced from Spain, the United States, and Japan, as well as having to deal with waves of Christian and Muslim missionaries throughout their history.

The fact that the animistic spirits are portrayed as female figures in the story highlights the role of women in the Philippines. Many spirit mediums or healers are women in the Philippines. The central role women play as healers is evident when the prince is "rescued" by Abadeha, the only person who is able to remove the destructive rings from his fingers. In the Indo-European versions of the Cinderella story, the female main character is "rescued" by a male of high social standing, such as a prince (Levi-Strauss, 1955). In contrast, *Abadeha* is a strikingly female-centric story.

Besides the Indo-European versions of Cinderella, especially the Disney film version that people from the United States are familiar with, the Plains Indian cultures of North America have a male version of Cinderella, *Ash Boy*. The Philippines's version of the Cinderella story contrasts both to the North American Plains Indian cultures and Indo-European versions of the story. Levi-Strauss (1955) notes that *Ash Boy* and "Cinderella are symmetrical but inverted in every detail" (p. 441).

That is, Ash Boy is a male, Cinderella is female; Ash Boy is ugly, Cinderella is beautiful; his ugliness is transformed by supernatural help, she receives beautiful clothing with the aid of supernatural assistance, and more. Again, Franz Boas's reference to myths being shattered and built up again with the shattered pieces seems relevant here to all three stories, *Abadeha*, *Ash Boy*, and *Cinderella*, which carry similar threads of meaning but are different in detail.

References

Boas, F. (1898). Introduction. In J. A. Teit, *Traditions of the Thompson River Indians of British Columbia: Collected and annotated* (pp. 1–18). Boston: The American Folklore Society by Houghton and Mifflin.

Levi-Strauss, C. (1955). The structural study of myth. *The Journal of American Folklore, 68*(270), 428–44.

Pan de Sal Saves the Day: A Filipino Children's Story, by Norma Olizon-Chikiamco. Illustrated by M. Salvatus. North Clarendon, VT: Tuttle Publishing, 2009.

Summary

A young girl named Pan de Sal is shy. She thinks she is ordinary, unlucky, and really doesn't like the way she looks. She is embarrassed for living in a poor, humble hut and for always eating simple foods. Pan de Sal envies her classmates Croissant, Muffin, Danish, Honey, and Super Bread, who are much richer; and she believes her classmates are much prettier and more interesting than her. She possesses none of the fancy things that her classmates have. However, Pan de Sal has a beautiful singing voice but lacks the confidence and courage to participate in the Glee Club.

One day on a class field trip, an unexpected event forces Pan de Sal to express herself and come into the limelight. She shows her classmates new things and gives them delicious and interesting food items for lunch. With talents revealed that she was unwilling and embarrassed to share before, she wins admiration from her classmates and finds the confidence to accept herself and fulfill her dreams.

Toward Authentic Interpretations

Pan de Sal Saves the Day is an inspiring story for children who have ever felt like outsiders. The characters are based on well-known pastries such as Croissant, Muffin, Danish, Honey, Super Bread, and Bread Sticks. The main character, Pan de Sal, is named after a famous Filipino pastry. If you know what Pan de Sal is, you would know the reason why this story uses this pastry as a character who is considered an outsider. Compared to well-known pastries that are sold worldwide, Pan de Sal is less known by people outside of Filipino culture. It is a simple yet very popular sweet bun eaten in the Philippines. Like the story's character, Pan de Sal seems plain and unappetizing, yet when you eat it you realize that it tastes wonderful.

Pastries such as the Croissant, Muffin, and Danish are known throughout the planet and are sold in many stores around the world. Pan de Sal (salt bread in English, or pandesal in the Philippines), on the other hand, is rarely seen in the United States. Most Filipinos make Pan de Sal at home and eat them with many meals, especially breakfast. As plain as they seem, they are popular in Filipino culture, but not so much elsewhere.

In the story the character Pan de Sal mentions many famous dishes that are made in the Filipino culture, such as "chicken Adobo." The Filipino dishes discussed by Pan de Sal contrast to the popular lunches her classmates bring, such as pizza, fried chicken, and spaghetti, all of which are eaten and marketed worldwide.

Readers should realize that the story symbolically traces the colonial history of the Philippines through the use of pastry. Spanish contact with the Philippines began with the arrival of Ferdinand Magellan in 1521, and the Spanish Colonial Era ended with the victory of the United States over Spain in the Spanish-American War of 1898. The United States ruled the Philippines until the start of World War II, when the American troops were overrun by the military forces of the Empire of Japan. When Japan was defeated at the end of war, the United States regained control of the Philippines.

The Philippines gained its formal independence from the United States in 1946 but served host to large US military bases for decades afterward. Before the arrival of the Spanish, the primary Filipino staple crop was rice. The Spanish brought with them wheat-based bread, which was the origin of Pan de Sal. When the United States defeated Spain and became the colonial rulers of the Philippines, the price of American wheat was cheaper than rice, making Pan de Sal a staple food for all Filipinos, rich and poor.

Pan de Sal may be plain and less known to peoples from other cultures, but it is a symbol of the resilience of the Filipino people, who have endured and overcome the oppression of foreign colonizers.

A Feast of Gold, by L. Romulo, in *Filipino Children's Favorite Stories*. Illustrated by J. de León. Hong Kong: Periplus, 2000.

Summary

There was a rich couple who owned a large farm and had a big house with many servants. They didn't care about the things they already owned or pursuing a life of comfort. All they cared about was money. From morning to night all they did was count their gold. One day a servant comes in to tell them that lunch is ready, but the rich man is not concerned about lunch; instead, he sends the servant away so he can continue counting his gold.

Hours later the couple finally comes to the kitchen to eat, but when they arrive they discover that all the food had turned into gold. Instead of being concerned about not having lunch, the rich couple are delighted to see more gold. They are excited to see that they are even richer than they thought, so they throw a celebration. As they prepare for the celebration, the chef notices that all the food in the pantry has also turned into gold. Still not worried about food, they squeal with excitement. The couple are so focused on the gold they forget about food and their hunger.

The couple does not eat, they do not sleep, and they even stop speaking to one another. As they get weaker, they continue to count their coins. The servants try to bring food from the outside, but anything that they bring into the rich couple's home turns into gold. The thought of stopping to count their gold coins to go outside and eat never occurs to them. Neither are able to break the spell of greed. Eventually both die from starvation, never having enjoyed their riches.

Toward Authentic Interpretations

The story *A Feast of Gold* has many different versions in other cultures, but all focus on the theme of greed. A similar story that is read in the United States is called *The Golden Feast*, which has the same basic story and theme.

In the Filipino version the greedy couple dies. The American version never directly mentions death but ends with the words "they never stepped outside their home again." This leaves the reader to decide what inevitably happens to the couple. Looking at children's literature in the United States, especially for young children ages K–4, authors tend to avoid directly mentioning death in their stories but imply that outcome.

Not speaking for all Filipino families, but many families in Filipino culture try to teach children not to be greedy. A family tries to take care of everyone within the family and even close friends. Although Filipinos are also taught to be independent, they are supported by their family. Filipinos value their family and relationships, and most Filipinos work hard to support them. In this regard, in most Filipinos' minds the value of relationships with friends and family is of greater value than any materialistic gain.

SOUTH KOREA, BY EUN YOO

The Tiger and the Dried Persimmon: A Korean Folk Tale, by J. J. Park. Toronto, Canada: Groundwood Books, 2002.

Summary

A tiger believed that he was the fiercest animal in the world and no one could challenge him. One day, he comes down the mountain and searches for food. It is dark when he arrives at a farmhouse. The tiger finds an ox sleeping in the shed. Then he hears a baby crying and a mother trying to soothe her child. The mother warns her infant that a wolf, a black bear, and a tiger are coming, so the baby needs to be quiet, but the baby still cries.

The mother then says, "OK, here is a persimmon," and gives her baby a piece of the dried fruit. The baby instantly stops crying. The tiger thinks that he has just discovered that persimmons are the fiercest animals, rather than a tiger, and decides to get as far away as he can from this dangerous creature.

At the same time, a thief arrives at the farmhouse and has come to steal the ox. In the darkness, the thief thinks that the tiger is the ox and leaps onto its back. The tiger thinks that a persimmon has jumped on its back and is so afraid that it runs and runs for hours, with the thief holding on until sunrise. In the morning light, the thief realizes that he is riding on a tiger's back. He grabs the branch of a tree and jumps off. With the thief off his back, the tiger feels that he has finally freed himself from the world's fiercest animal. He never again goes down to the village where the dried persimmon lives.

Toward Authentic Interpretations

In order to understand the humor the story portrays, readers must know the significant meaning persimmons hold in Korean culture and some other Asian cultures.

Although persimmons are eaten in Western countries, people throughout Asia probably love persimmons, both ripe and dried, even more. Before persimmons are ripe, they are green and bitter. However, when ripe they change color to a vibrant orange and are very sweet, round with a flat bottom, and have a crunchy, fragrant flavor. In Buddhism, persimmons symbolize transformation. Green persimmons are acrid and bitter—meaning immature and ignorant—but they transform into sweet fruit—mature and wise. In other words, persimmons are used as a metaphor for becoming a better person through education.

Because the image of tigers as big, strong, and scary is taken for granted, the portrayal of a tiger in the story as timid and afraid of a small persimmon becomes humorous. The fact that tigers and persimmons share the same color—orange—adds to the humor. The story's implicit moral is that it is essential to judge a situation with wise eyes and a sensible mind, a fundamental perspective of Buddhist teaching.

Teachers could bring persimmons to class, ask the children to describe them, and perhaps even let them take a little bite of a slice of ripe persimmon (or dried persimmon like in the story) to see what it tastes like (depending on the rules of the school). If the children can't sample it, at least they could see a persimmon and be told that the fruit is sweet and tasty. Then proceed with the story.

The Green Frogs: A Korean Folk Tale, by Yumi Heo. New York: Houghton Mifflin, 1996.

Summary

A long time ago, there were two green frogs, both boys, who loved disobeying their mother. They always did the opposite of what she told them to do. When their mother finished cooking she would ask them to sit down and eat, but the two green frogs would giggle, hop around, and play with their spoons. When their mother told them to clean up their mess, the two green frogs would ignore her and jump up and down on their chairs.

One day she taught them how to croak, "CROAK! CROAK! CROAK!" But the two green frogs were so naughty they croaked backward, "KA-ORC! KA-ORC! KA-ORC!" Afterward, if she wanted to have quiet time and read a book, they would immediately begin croaking backward, "KA-ORC! KA-ORC! KA-ORC!" They gave her no peace. When the frog mother called out to her sons, "Don't get dirty!" the two green frogs would jump into the muddy end of the pond almost as soon as the words left her mouth. Whatever their mother said the green frogs would do the opposite.

Time passes and the mother frog becomes old and sick and decides she wants to be buried on the sunny side of the hill. However, she knows that her two green frog sons always do the opposite of what she tells them, so she asks her sons to bury her in the shade by the stream instead.

After mother frog died, her sons feel sad and are sorry that they never listened to her. They decide to obey her for the first time and bury her by the stream as she told them. Soon afterward it began raining for days and nights, and the stream overflows its banks. The green frogs began to worry that their mother's grave will wash away. They go to the stream, and for the first time they croak just like their mother had taught them, "CROAK! CROAK! CROAK!" They beg the stream not to wash away their mother's grave. Since then, whenever it rains, green frogs sit by streams and cry out, "CROAK! CROAK! CROAK!"

Toward Authentic Interpretations

In order to understand this story, readers need to know about Korean culture. For centuries Korean culture has been influenced by the teachings of Confucius, a teacher and philosopher who lived in China 2,500 years ago. Confucian culture emphasizes the importance of filial piety; that is, respecting parents and elders. Korean people are encouraged to be respectful to their elders and listen to the guidance of parents.

The story of *The Green Frogs* is told to children to discourage misbehavior and to emphasize the importance of filial piety. In Korea when parents or other people encounter a misbehaving child they call the child "a green frog." When teachers in the United States read this story to students, teachers can explain the importance of respecting parents, both in Korea and the United States. After reading this book, students can think about how they relate to their own parents and guardians.

To understand more about Korea and Confucianism, students can also discuss why the naughty frogs are boys in this story. Where are the girl frogs? Confucianism emphasizes males over females, but the story only mentions the female parent of the naughty frogs. Where is the daddy frog in the story? How would the naughty boy frogs act if their daddy was around?

In the Moonlight Mist: A Korean Folk Tale, by Daniel San Souci. Honesdale, PA: Boyds Mill Press, 1999.

Summary

One spring afternoon, a young woodcutter hears a loud crackling in the distant underbrush. A deer comes to ask help to run away from a hunter. The woodcutter leads the deer behind a pile of wood and covers him with branches and leaves, thus saving the deer's life. The deer asks what the woodcutter's wish is, and he says that he has always dreamed of having a loving wife and children of his own, but he is poor and could barely take care of his old mother and himself. The deer says that his wish will be granted and gives him information about what he needs to do.

The deer tells the woodcutter to climb to the crest of the mountain where he will see a lake at the first full moon. This was a unique lake, where heavenly maidens bathe under the full moon. While the maidens are bathing, the woodcutter is told that he should snatch one set of clothes from a heavenly maiden, for without her clothes the maiden will not be able to return to heaven. At the same time, she will see the goodness in him and will become his earthly wife. The deer also warns the woodcutter not to give back his wife's heavenly clothes until she bears him a second child.

When a full moon appears over the mountain, the woodcutter follows the path all the way to the crest of the mountain. Finally, he finds a lake that looks like a giant mirror, reflecting the moon and stars. The woodcutter hides behind a large rock near the shore. He sees that there are beautiful maidens floating downward through the moonlit mist. Once they land on shore, they hang their clothes on the lowest limb of a willow tree. While the maidens are swimming out to the middle of the lake, the woodcutter removes one set of the radiant clothes. One maiden cannot find her clothes and cannot return to heaven. The earth-bound maiden weeps sadly, and the woodcutter says that he will take care of her. She is frightened at first, but because the woodcutter seems so kind and concerned she decides to go home with him. Soon she falls in love with him, and the two are married and have a baby.

Although she is happy with her earthly life, she misses her home in heaven. She wants to see her heavenly clothes, and he shows them to her. She became spellbound by the power they possess and puts them on. Soon she and the baby are floating up in to the sky and vanish completely. The woodcutter's life becomes miserable, and when he goes out to get food he meets the deer. The deer says when the moon is full, the heavenly maidens lower a silver bucket into the lake to fill with water for their baths. The deer instructs the woodcutter to go to the lake that night, climb inside the bucket, and be lifted to heaven and reunited with his wife and child.

The woodcutter wants to take his mother to heaven with him. When the bucket is lowered, he puts his mother inside first and then climbs in. The bucket starts to rise but comes to a sudden halt. The woodcutter jumps out of the bucket and watches as his mother is lifted to heaven. When the heavenly king hears the story of how the woodcutter sacrificed his own happiness for his mother's well-being, he sends a dragon-horse to bring the woodcutter to heaven. The woodcutter is soon reunited with his family, and their joy gives the moon and stars a luster.

Toward Authentic Interpretations

In order to comprehend this story, it is important to understand that respecting parents is extremely important in Korean culture. Because the heavenly king respects the sacrifices the woodcutter makes for his mother, he makes it possible for the woodcutter to be reunited with his entire family in heaven. Many Korean tales include a form of poetic justice, where kindness and virtue are rewarded, such as another instance in the story where the impoverished woodcutter saves the life of a deer and the deer is able to repay him by helping him meet and marry a heavenly maiden.

When teachers read this story to students, they can explain virtue and poetic justice as it is conceived by Koreans, a people influenced by Confucianism and Buddhism. After reading this book, students can discuss the good deeds they have done or plan to do for their parents, grandparents, siblings, and friends.

THAILAND, BY KAMOLWAN FAIREE JOCUNS

Tua and the Elephant, by R. P. Harris. San Francisco: Chronicle Books, 2012.

Summary

Tua and the Elephant by R. P. Harris tells a story about a girl, Tua, who lives in Chiangmai, a province in the north of Thailand, and a young elephant that is later named Pohn-Pohn. One day when Tua goes to the market, she discovers that an elephant is being abused by mahouts (trainers) in an elephant show. After the show she follows them to the river, where they take a rest and stay overnight. She rescues the elephant and brings it to her aunt's home, and then begins a series of adventures to help the elephant escape from the mahouts. With the help of the monk at the temple, she finds an elephant sanctuary where the elephant eventually finds peace.

Classroom Applications

Elephants are known as *Sat-Khu-Baan-Khu-Mueng*, are the national animal of Thailand, and were used during warfare in Thailand when they fought alongside kings. One could say it is an honorable and much revered animal, especially white elephants that were represented on the Thai national flag from 1820 to 1971.

Nowadays, though the elephant has disappeared from the Thai national flag, it is still valued in Thai society. Thai elephants are used in commercial images for Thai tourism and businesses. Their images have been used in TV commercials as well as in souvenirs and other goods. However, there is also a dark side in how elephants are used.

The issue underlying this story concerns both abuse of the elephant as well as its ownership. In the story it is mentioned that a mahout owns the elephant. Although elephants are one of the animals on Thailand's wildlife protection list, some elephants, such as the one in the story, are registered as domestic elephants and can be legally owned. A wild elephant or elephant parts such as tusks cannot be owned or traded. Even though the mahouts claimed that they had a license, it does not mean they can do whatever they so wish to do with the elephant. Abuse of either wild elephants or domesticated elephants is illegal in Thailand. From a Thai perspective, Tua made the correct decision in trying to bring Pohn-Pohn to an elephant sanctuary where it will be taken care of properly, trained, and live safely. Returning domesticated elephants to the forest might not be a good decision as it had been raised differently from wild elephants and thus might not survive there. This book helps to raise concerns about animal abuse and is useful for discussing how elephants can serve as a significant cultural symbol for a country like Thailand, apart from being exploited for gross commercial gains.

A Child of the Northeast, by Kampoon Bunthawi. Translated by Susan Fulop Kepner. Bangkok, Thailand: Duang Kamol, 1988.

Summary

A Child of the Northeast was written by Kampoon Boontawee and won the South East Asia Write Award in 1976. The book was translated into English by

Susan Fulop Kepner. The story is about Koon, an eight-year-old boy, and his rural village life in the northeast of Thailand during 1930s and the Depression.

One day in the dry season when Koon's family knew that they would have just enough rice to last for the next five months, they decide to make a trek from their village for a few days with other families in order to fish in a river. Koon is allowed to join them on their journey. He is extremely excited and learns much about things outside of his village.

Toward Authentic Interpretations

The story is set in the northeast of Thailand, which is called *Isan*. It is a part of Thailand that is far from the ocean, and it is one of the driest parts of the country during the dry season. This region is large, and most of the land is used for agriculture, especially wet rice farming. However, rice cannot be planted all year round and needs much water. During the dry season or during draught years rice farmers cannot grow rice, or they might only have low yields from their harvests. This is the reason why Koon's family had to set out to fish in a river far from home.

The story shows how rice is an important part of the Thai diet. Koon's family had to start a journey to fish in the river because they would soon be short of rice. During the Depression in rural Thailand, this puts them in a precarious situation. In deciding to catch fish they could both augment their diet and sell or trade fish or fish byproducts for rice in the city. For the book's characters, a meal was not considered complete without rice since it is a good source of carbohydrates and for subsistence. It is sometimes the only source for rice farmers.

Although this book focuses specifically on poor rice farmers in rural Thailand during the 1930s, it can help students understand that people in many parts of the world have needed to struggle to overcome the harsh conditions imposed by the circumstances of their lives.

Kaew the Playful, by Princess Maha Chakri Sirindhorn, HRH. Translated by Sumalee. Bangkok, Thailand: Nanmeebooks, 2014.

Summary

Kaew the Playful is a fictional tale for children written by Waen Kaew, the pen name for H. R. H., Princess Maha Chakri Sirindhorn. It was translated into English by Sumalee. The story is about Kaew, a student in grade four. The book contains a collection of short stories of Kaew's everyday adventures, most of which involve her getting into trouble. For example, in the chapter "Career Training," Kaew decides that she wants to be a nurse when she grows up, but she finds that it is difficult to get herself ready for that while she is still young, unlike other children who want to be a teacher and can practice by tutoring friends, or those who want to be a fashion designer can practice drawing or sewing.

Kaew comes up with a plan. She decides to ride a bicycle really fast so that she will fall and get injured. In that way she can do first-aid training, but her plan goes awry as she injures herself more seriously than she had intended and has to go to the doctor.

Classroom Applications

The chapter also describes how Kai, Kaew's sister, wants to be a teacher and her parents are proud of her because she will be "a mold of the nation." This is a Thai phrase that regards teachers as people who nurture and pass their knowledge on to students. They mold a nation by being immensely influential to students, the future of the country. If students have a good teacher, they tend to be good like their teacher.

The chapter "Career Training" is a good one for discussing the roles of different jobs, how they are important to society, and how students have varying attitudes toward different professions. The chapter also indicates the intercultural value of teachers in other cultures. Teachers can also use other chapters in the book to explore topics such as the folk beliefs of students from other cultures. Such chapters include: "A Rainy Night," "The Moon Was Eaten," "Séance," and "A Ghost of an Old Chinese Man."

About the Editors

Daniel Miles Amos was the first US graduate student to successfully complete ethnographic research in the People's Republic of China. He has been professionally affiliated with several universities in Asia and the United States, including the Chinese University of Hong Kong, Beijing Normal University, Wuhan University, Clark Atlanta University, and the University of Washington. Currently, he is a Fulbright Scholar completing research in Hong Kong.

Yukari Takimoto Amos, a native of Japan, is a professor of multicultural education and TESL at Central Washington University. She has published journal articles, book chapters, and books on a wide range of subjects. Her research has included studies of Asian international students, teacher candidates of color, critical race theory, and ESL/JSL (Japanese as a Second Language) pedagogy.

About the Contributors

Anita Balagopalan has more than seventeen years of experience in television production, having worked as a producer, anchor, and correspondent at one of India's leading television networks, Network18. She also ran her own production house in Mumbai for two years. Now based in Hong Kong, she works as a freelance scriptwriter for a few special series on infotainment and TV news channels and corporate films. She has also been creating social media and digital content for small businesses and start-ups based in Hong Kong and India for the last two years. Anita is currently involved with a social enterprise based in India, CrossBow Miles, as the head of Social Media & Communications.

Kamolwan Fairee Jocuns holds a master of science degree in teaching English to speakers of other languages from the University of Edinburgh. She is currently a lecturer at the Department of English and Linguistics, Thammasat University, Bangkok, Thailand. Her research interests include children's literature, young adult literature, and English language teaching.

Trina Lanegan holds an M.Ed and is an educator with twenty-three years of experience teaching at elementary, middle, and secondary levels. Her professional focus is on second language acquisition methodology and teacher training. Currently she is the early learning coordinator for the Ellensburg School District in Washington state.

Haiyue (Fiona) Shan is native Chinese and holds a master's degree in Chinese linguistics. She currently serves as a researcher at the University of Hong Kong. Her research interests include health care, migrants, TCSL (teaching Chinese as a second language), and second language acquisition. She has taught beginning and advanced level Chinese, contrastive analysis between Chinese and English, and creative writing.

ANNOTATED BIBLIOGRAPHY CONTRIBUTORS

Miao Ying (Janet) Chen was born in Taiwan. She completed a bachelor's degree in elementary education and TESL/bilingual education. Miao Ying has a passion for teaching ELLs and introducing different cultures to her students.

Tati Lathipatud Durriyah (Tati D. Wardi) is a lecturer at the Universitas Islam Negeri in Jakarta, Indonesia. Among many courses she teaches, her favorite one is an introduction to children's literature. Her classroom-based research focuses on reader response, picture books, and digital literacy. She loves talking about books and making a deliberate effort to develop a culture of reading with her student teachers.

Yae Takimoto Hite was born and raised in Japan through high school. Upon graduation, she moved to the United States. Yae holds a bachelor's degree in instructional foundations and bilingual/TESL education.

Katrina Manami Knight is a doctoral student in history at Emory University, and holds degrees in classical studies and archaeology from Tulane University and the University of Leicester.

Jordan Piano is a Filipino American teacher candidate at Central Washington University.

Eun Yoo is an ELL teacher at Kent Valley Early Learning Center in Kent, Washington. Before moving to the United States, she taught high school in South Korea. She loves to read children's literature books and uses them in her classroom.

www.ingramcontent.com/pod-product-compliance
Lightning Source LLC
Chambersburg PA
CBHW021800230426
43669CB00006B/148